AF281236

AMAYA LOWELL

DON'T LOOK BACK

A REWIKAN EMPIRE NOVEL
THE BEGINNER TRILOGY BOOK 1

Don't Look Back

Copyright

© 2025 Amaya Lowell

Translated from the German by Amaya Lowell.

Publisher: BoD · Books on Demand GmbH,

Überseering 33, 22297 Hamburg, bod@bod.de

ISBN: 978-3-8192-6568-6

Printed by: Libri Plureos GmbH, Friedensallee 273, 22763 Hamburg, Germany

First Edition, June 2025

Cover design: Mariella Lowell

Illustrations: Selin Junger

This is a work of fiction. All characters, names, places, and incidents are the product of the author's imagination. Any resemblance to actual persons, living or dead, or actual events is purely coincidental. The story is set in Asheville, North Carolina, USA.

Connect with the author:

Instagram: @amayalowellauthor

TikTok: @amayalowell

Website: bio.site/lowellworld

Note on the English Edition

This novel was originally written in German and translated into English using DeepL as a linguistic base. Every chapter was then manually revised, restructured and stylistically refined by the author.

This is not an AI-written book. No content or creative scenes were generated using artificial intelligence. The author used AI strictly as a tool for linguistic support in translation, not for writing.

Mix-CD

Folsom Prison Blues - Johnny Cash
So Anxious - Ginuwine
Play That Funky Music - Wild Cherry
Sex & Candy - Marcy Playground
The Way You Make Me Feel - Michael Jackson
Kiss - Prince
Do You Wanna Touch Me (Oh Yeah) - Joan Jett & the
Blackhearts
I Love Rock'N Roll - Joan Jett & the Blackhearts
You Give Love A Bad Name - Bon Jovi
What a Girl Wants - Christina Aguilera
Waterfalls - TLC
I Touch Myself - Divinyls
Proud Mary - Tina Turner
Sex on Fire - Kings of Leon

Wake Me Up Before You Go-Go - Wham!

This Is How We Do It - Montell Jordan, Wino

Stop - Spice Girls

Authors Note

Warning: This book may contain content that is not suitable for all readers. It contains dark themes, explicit scenes and mental health issues. Recommended for ages 18+.

Don't Look Back is a story set in the Rewikan Empire and is not part of one of the main series, so can be read as a standalone.

It is set in Asheville, a small town in the US state of North Carolina.

On page 209 you will find a list of explicit content - possible spoilers!

Lots of love,

Amy

Freedom

1

Cassettes and ties

Marra

'm trudging through the tall grass in my cowboy boots, bootcut jeans, a full basket and a raised hand in front of my eyes. My beautiful red, and incredibly expensive, '98 Dodge Ram 1500 Quad Cab is parked on the side of the road, bathed in a beautiful light of red, yellow and orange from the setting sun.

My father didn't give me much leeway when it came to choosing my own car.

At first I drove his old K5 Blazer because he didn't have enough money to buy me a "girl's car" after I graduated from high school.

His words, not mine. But when the time came for me to get my first car - *he* decided for me. He thought the Dodge suited me perfectly: rustic, reliable, a few scratches but loved. And I still don't know whether that's a compliment or an insult.

But my dad was right, I love my Dodge. It has a gray cloth upholstery and still smells a bit like cigarettes from the previous owner. Cranking the windows can be exhausting, but it's always worth it when the wind blows through my hair afterwards. But what I like best is the rumbling sound when it starts - sometimes it takes several attempts.

Sighing, I drop into the driver's seat, pull the door shut, which squeaks into the lock, insert a new cassette into the deck - *Johnny Cash* with "Folsom Prison Blues" - and let the engine roar to life.

My little red tank, not particularly pretty but *mine*.

Before I set off, I carefully place the basket on the back seat and check once again that I have everything I need.

I can use the flowers I've collected to make wreaths for Miss Jolly, who has booked me for her granddaughter's birthday. My little craft sells well, albeit slowly at first. I'm glad I live near the forest and have enough resources to get by most of the time and not have to reorder anything.

I drive home, where Leo - my cat - is already waiting for me, purring and meowing, and when I arrive in the kitchen I pop in the next cassette so that "So Anxious" by *Ginuwine* is blaring through my apartment.

Humming, I tidy up the things I left lying all over the place this morning, give Leo a few treats and then go to my tiny closet. I really couldn't have picked a worse one. But before I moved into my new apartment, I lived in a tiny one in Asheville. With a roommate.

Moving out of Asheville and finding something cute and small in the quiet town of Weaverville was the best idea that came to mind. Asheville is also very quiet and close to nature, but there is more hustle and bustle there than here.

However, today is our annual class reunion where everyone finds the time to get together. Most of the time these reunions are totally lame and a waste of time, but I still do them every year.

And that's why I need something decent to wear.

Leo can spend the evening alone and I suspect I won't be gone long either way.

Old school parties are always dull.

When I leave the house, I'm wearing an eye-catching pleated top in a bright, summery yellow that makes my sun-kissed skin glow. It's figure-hugging and ends just above my waist, and I've paired it with short, dark blue jeans that look smart but not too overdressed for a night out. My white, high boots add the finishing touch to my outfit and I feel really confident again for the first time in a long time. I rarely dress up for anything, but even my face is adorned with frosty eyeshadow and pale pink lipstick. My hair falls in soft waves over my shoulders and I wear rings and bracelets. I hope I don't look too over the top and extreme, but I guess some of my old classmates will look a lot worse. One thing I can't miss, though: my bag, which contains more bits and bobs than my Great Aunt Rose's bedside drawer. It's not perfect - from lip balm to crumpled receipts and old hair clips - but that's why it suits me.

Probably just like the Dodge.

The drive doesn't take long, only about 15 minutes, and then I'm already standing in front of the restaurant I've been invited to tonight.

The memories of my school days fluctuate between frustration and humor.

Small groups are already gathering outside the front door and I notice people I would rather not see.

But I also recognize my old school friend Elara, a Western European beauty with short-cropped brown hair, tanned skin and chocolate-colored eyes.

Sighing, I get out, pull my bag behind me and greet my old friend.

She tells me about her new job in Chicago, about the man she met and married there, but who unfortunately can't be here today - there's too much to do at work. I also chat briefly with a few others, Owen, an old classmate and humorous guy, sits down next to me when we find our seats in the restaurant's common room.

His blond hair hangs a little in his eyes and he keeps running his fingers through his hair, like an uncontrollable tic, as we talk about the last years in Asheville. He divorced his wife a few weeks ago and took custody of his two sons, who are now staying with a friend.

"And you?"

The question catches me off guard. He knows that I no longer live in this area. When I moved, I had hoped that they would think I was doing it because of a man.

But that's absolutely not the case. "I've opened a small event and party service and got myself a cat," I begin, "his name is Leo." I immediately feel like a retarded child, but Owen smiles gently at me. I suppose it's better than having a failed marriage and being a single dad.

As the food is served, I look through the other rows of tables and notice three men dressed more finely and expensively than the others. At that moment, I feel strange in my outfit.

I take a closer look and recognize them.

The suits must be expensive. The way they have rolled up the white sleeves of their shirts and are wearing a tie around their necks... they look like they're not from around here.

But I know better - I went to school with them for many years.

Layton Reed, Jasper Bailey and Valerian King.

"I've noticed them too," Owen says, leaning over to me, "weird, right?"

They haven't shown up at a reunion in years. They haven't shown up since they turned their backs on Asheville. Why would they? They've obviously built something big.

Dana, the girl sitting next to me like in the old school days, joins in the conversation and leans over to us. With her fork to her lip, she starts to grin.

"They were in the local paper - they've really made it big and earned a lot of money." The rest of the evening passes quietly, unpacking old stories and reminiscing as if it were only yesterday. Owen and Dana bicker and provoke each other, but it's entertaining and funny. They were the same back then.

A couple of old classmates give a speech and we get treated to something new, with me also having my glass refilled at every opportunity. I can't avoid looking over at the three men, who seem to be very introverted. They only chat here and there with people in their seating area and otherwise concentrate on the food and the program on offer in the middle of the room. If there are no speeches, then there are little dance interludes and games that we used to play.

I keep a low profile and stay glued to my chair. It's also much easier to watch from my position anyway.

Layton and I used to get on well and were even close friends in private. The older we got, the further apart we grew, but we stayed in touch through school and often talked or joked with each other.

However, I had very little to do with Valerian and Jasper. Apart from computer science lessons, which I enjoyed with all three of them, I only knew Jasper and Valerian from geography lessons.

I lick my lips and take another sip of the champagne they offer us.

Thoughtful and lost in old memories, I finish my dessert when the chair next to me is pulled back and Layton sits down next to me. I immediately start to grin. He still has his strawberry-honey blonde hair, which curls slightly, and the amber eyes.

As my gaze moves from his pointed smile down to his hands, I notice the silver ring he's always worn before. He looks different and familiar at the same time.

A little wider and taller, firmer and more serious.

Damn attractive.

A soft warmth rises in my cheeks as I notice the sparkle in his eyes when he looks at me. How long has it been? Far too long, and strangely, it feels like he's never been away and like he's sitting next to me every day. At the same time, it robs me of the ability to breathe properly.

"We haven't seen each other for a long time, Mar." When he calls me by my old, now extinct nickname, my heart warms, but I return his wide grin. "Looks like you had a good time," I say and he nods faintly. He runs a hand through his hair and blinks a few times. "Yeah, we made good use of the time. It's nice to see you again."

"I hope so, who isn't happy to see me?"

I can't help but notice that the others at the table glance at us, and Jasper and Valerian seem to have noticed me too, but they stay in their seats.

Layton picks up on my joke and winks at me.

"Of course I'm only here because of you, dearest Marra. The last few years have been very lonely without you."

My heart pounds against my chest, even though he's only saying it as a joke.

It's just a joke.

A joke.

"It must have been like rehab," I continue, and Layton laughs. His mouth twists in the same way as before, only controlled, but his upper body quivers as if he's trying to hold it back a little.

Then he shakes his head. "You haven't changed at all, Marra."

I shrug my shoulders. "The real deal."

I enjoy joking with him again and exchanging some news. I ask him about a few old acquaintances he probably has more to do with than me, and when he's finished his water, he politely says goodbye to me and goes back to his seat.

Dana slowly creeps back after returning from the restroom and gives me a conspiratorial look. "What was that all about?" She knows there was a spark between me and Layton once, when we were much younger, but it never turned into anything more.

His eyes have always made my knees weak, just like his cheeky grin and sweet nature. I remember lying with my head on his chest and him running his fingers soothingly over my hair when I was stoned and tired while we enjoyed time with friends. Everyone went to find a room, but I crawled into bed with him and we talked all night long.

That was the first and last time we got that close.

With my cheeks flushed with inner heat, I spend the next few minutes trying to steer the conversation between Dana, Owen and I onto something else and avoiding Layton's gaze. I wonder if he remembers.

As more and more people get ready to leave, I get up from my chair and say goodbye to my old friends. It was nice to see them again and I have to admit that the evening didn't go as badly as I had expected. It wasn't nearly as boring as the last few times either, because this time we had some exciting guests.

I cast a sideways glance at Layton's seat, but realize that he's no longer there, nor is Valerian, and only Jasper is sitting there, staring at his little push-button phone.

"Maybe, if you feel like it, we can see each other more often now?" I turn my gaze to Owen, who is gradually getting ready to go home to his sons. "Yes, why not. I'd love to," I accept his offer and hug him one last time before making my way to the exit of the hall.

Yawning, I walk through the decorated hallway, thank the nice waiters from tonight as I pass by and then push the door open with a sigh.

I wipe my face, walk down the few steps and am scared to death when I see the man staring hungrily and darkly into my eyes.

2

The baksetball player

Marra

*I*n the meantime, Valerian has taken off his suit jacket and hung it over the seat of the black Harley, against which he leans and smokes. He looks at me as if he's trying to solve a riddle and tilts his head, causing my stomach to flip upside down and do a few loops.

My goodness, was this guy this hot before?

The music from the restaurant radio trills out to us through a couple of open windows, and I have to smile gently as I recognize the song. It's "Play That Funky Music" by *Wild Cherry*.

Cigarette smoke rises into the cool evening air and his dark blue eyes look focused - seeing only me.

His light blond hair is tousled and untamed. He used to wear caps, but today he stands here, the tailored suit, the narrow pants - a clear statement against his old world. His cigarette glows as he takes another drag. It is already dark and only the lights of the restaurant let me recognize him.

Unsure whether I should say anything to him - after all, it would be the first time in many years - I just keep walking and try to get past him. The way he looks at me eats holes in my body and it feels like he's sucking my whole existence out of me.

When I'm level with him, he stands up straight and lets off his motorcycle. My heart beats from my chest into my head so that I can feel it pounding against my skull, and I blink nervously at him.

Valerian is the type of man who can do anything and look sexy as hell doing it. He could walk around shirtless, with a scarf wrapped around his head and shorts, and no one would think to look askance at him, because everything else about him... is just about perfect.

I can't put into words exactly what it is. The little moles on his face that come together like a work of art and make him unique? The piercing eyes in combination with his thin but always amused lips? The straight nose that tapers towards the end? His body, which is perhaps not as broad as Layton's and rather narrower, but still athletic and attractive? Or his charisma and posture, which is dark, cold and at the same time attractive and appealing?

Whatever it is, I get incredibly hot when he's still looking at me and doesn't even seem to blink.

I stop next to him.

I don't know why, but it's a reaction from my body that I simply have no control over.

"You look even better than you did then," he says. His voice has become deeper, rougher. I almost choke on the thin air as I realize the meaning of his words.

I bite my lower lip and grip my bag tighter with my fingers. "Is that supposed to be a compliment?"

He throws his cigarette butt on the floor and slides his hands into his pants pockets. Seeing him in this suit somehow doesn't suit him at all. It looks like he's wearing a shell.

"I've always thought you were hot," he admits, and my cheeks glow. I shift my weight to the other leg and hold my breath in surprise.

I want to ask him how he can say that so openly and directly, but how do you ask something like that? But I don't even get a chance, because then he continues. "There's no reason not to tell you. I might not have dared back then, but there's nothing wrong with it now, is there, little Mar? I'll be on a plane back to New York in a few hours." I swallow.

Excuse me?

Is he completely out of his mind?

"What are you getting at? A one-night stand?"

I've never really known what he thinks of me. Valerian would give me the occasional glance in class, watching me when he thought I wouldn't notice. My heart has run a marathon every time I've caught even a hint of his attention.

He laughs softly and harshly, shaking his head in amusement. "I'm just being honest with you, little one. But even if I was up for a one-night stand with you, would that be a bad thing?"

He comes closer to me, so that his breath almost touches my skin, and I could scream in frustration when it doesn't.

Where are these old feelings coming from all of a sudden?

"I don't get into bed with strange men."

A weak statement - but I can't think of anything better.

After leaving school, I completely forgot about them and never looked back - just like the three of them. Class reunions are the only thing I attend, and probably only to get upset about it later.

But he, just like Layton and Jasper, has never been there.

And now I spend an evening in the same room as these three men and all my darkest desires come flooding back?

Maybe I'm the one who's lost my mind, too.

His right eye twitches.

"That's probably for the best. But we're not strangers and you know it."

"If we're not strangers, even though we haven't seen each other in at least six years, then what are we?" He doesn't answer me directly, scrutinizing my face, and I wonder if he can hear my rapidly beating heart.

His unashamed beauty distracts me from the thought that I actually wanted to go home long ago, and the courage behind this conversation makes me feel pure pride.

"Old acquaintances. Two souls who know each other well and are meeting again after a long time, little Mar." I feel like I'm 18 again and like those effervescent feelings never went away, but then he comes even closer to me, closer than ever, and I can see the little dark spots in his blue eyes. "I bet you're dirtier than you act."

Speechless and completely dumbfounded, I look at him. His lips twist into a cynical, beautiful smile, his eyes shining, and I feel like he's captivating me with it. With just one smile, he manages to capture all my attention. Suddenly he's even closer, putting an arm around my waist and pulling me towards him.

I gasp and hold on to his shoulders, the tips of our noses gently touching. He's searching for something in my eyes, but I'm not quite sure what. I don't know if he'll find what he's looking for.

"And I bet you think I'm just as hot as I used to be." I feel his hands dig into my skin and our warm bodies snuggle together.

When I gently shake my head, his eyes darken and he tilts his head slightly.

Just fuck it.

Go all in, Marra.

"No. Even hotter than before," I whisper.

This man is the epitome of pure attraction and appeal.

In the next moment, his mouth captures mine and I wrap my arms around his neck. I could swear that my heart is going to explode at any moment and the pulsation of lust inside me will increase immeasurably.

It feels like someone has poured a can of gasoline inside me and lit it on fire - I'm doing something I dreamed of as a young girl and thought I'd never achieve.

I never dared to approach him about this attraction, I wished I could but I knew Valerian King wasn't into relationships. So why with me then?

And yet, almost seven years later, I'm standing in his arms, his lips pressed against mine and our bodies nestled close together.

I'm getting wet and can feel his trousers bulging at my crotch and pressing hard against me. Gasping, I break off the kiss only to meet his intense, hungry gaze, which makes me slide even deeper into his arms.

I have no idea what's wrong with me or why I'm doing this. I've never done anything like this before.

But I don't give a shit at the moment.

There's no place I'd rather be than here.

Our lips meet again and when his tongue brushes against my teeth, I let him explore my mouth. My hands move into his hair and I claw into it, his fingers grip me tighter, he leans down further, getting faster, more intense. Our tongues circle each other, our breath is almost exhausted, but we just keep going.

His hand slides to my ass and he holds it tight, the other reaches into my hair and pulls my head back.

It is a fire that ignites inside me. And it's looking for oxygen, mixed with adrenaline.

I squeeze my thighs together to escape the wetness and the tingling, but it's no use. Breathing heavily, we look at each other and I start to smile broadly.

Bloody hell.

"That alone was worth putting on this shitty suit and being dragged here. The only moment that doesn't feel like a waste of time. You're the only reason I'd willingly come back to this dump." I can hear the arousal in his raspy voice and I have to squint my eyes to keep from pouncing on him again.

What the hell is wrong with me?

"Shit, even me made that horny."

I jerk away from Valerian and look towards the entrance of the restaurant, where Jasper is leaning against the wall with a cigarette in his mouth, looking at us. Has he been watching us the whole time?

Fuck.

I laugh nervously and take a few more steps back, but Valerian stops me, grabs my hand and pulls me close again. "Don't be shy, little Mar," he whispers in my ear, but I look back and forth between him and Jasper. "He was here the whole time."

"And what did he see? That we're having fun together? You have nothing to be ashamed of, I bet he still has perverted thoughts in his little head."

He pulls me behind him and I guess I just let it happen because I'm too overwhelmed to resist. We join Jasper on the restaurant's veranda and I lean against the railing to at least get some distance and take a deep breath.

"I didn't mean to make you feel uncomfortable," I hear Jasper say, and I lift my gaze - look at him hesitantly.

Jasper Bailey in a suit looks like a music video playing on MTV while you eat chips out of a bag and wonder if this is your life right now.

He's huge. Like someone who plays basketball but doesn't talk about it much. His brown hair is sticking out in all directions, tousled as always, like the wind has been playing spin the bottle with him. But his brown eyes are still the same - warm and loyal - and as they look at me for a moment, I forget that he's not standing in front of me in his usual jeans and loose-fitting tank top. Instead, he's wearing the same suit, his tie loosely tied as if he's about to rip it off his neck at any moment.

He looks good, far too good.

Still, he looks like he'd rather throw himself back into his comfy shorts, with a smile that can say "I don't take you seriously" and "I'd go to war for you" at the same time.

"It's alright, I guess." Valerian lights another cigarette and offers me one, but I quickly decline.

I look back and forth between the two men in front of me.

I should go home.

Yes, I should do that.

But I feel like I'm stuck to the railing and their intense, engaging gazes are holding me.

Overwhelmed, I rub my bare arms.

"When's Lay coming?" Valerian turns to his friend, who shrugs his shoulders and takes another drag. "Should be out soon. He seems to have even less desire to sit here among the idiots since Marra left the hall."

I swallow at his words, look to the lanterns and blink.

I know his words were meant to get my attention - and they worked.

"How come you've never been here in the last few years," I say without looking at them, "if you don't mind me asking."

Valerian blows out a puff of smoke and grins crookedly. "There's nothing here for us." Jasper gives him a warning look, which he skillfully ignores.

"Lay and Val were planning to run off and build a career months before we graduated. When Jadie and I broke up, I didn't think twice and went with them. And it's not easy to build a business, even with three people. But it worked out."

Yes, and quite well, I see. Valerian wears an expensive watch on his left wrist, and even if he doesn't really like the suit, it's still very expensive. Not that I know anything about it, but I know that my father had to save forever for my degree to be able to afford a suit.

"I guess the crash course for stocks in computer science helped after all," I joke, hoping I'm not getting completely off topic. But Valerian grins even wider at my words and Jasper nods slightly with a laugh. "I suppose you could say that. Kings Strategies, the company, is all about stocks and finance. We play chess with the financial market, not poker. Val comes up with strategies, Lay reads the numbers, and I... well, I make sure the place runs. We help the rich get richer and earn more than is good for us. But it's also incredibly time-consuming. Even if we had wanted to, we simply wouldn't have had time to visit Asheville."

"Which we definitely didn't wanted - visiting Asheville, I mean. It's terrible here. We don't even have a place to stay for the night," Valerian interrupts him and throws his cigarette over the railing into the flower bed.

"Then why are you here?" I ask. I don't even go into the whole financial thing because I don't understand half of what Jasper is trying to explain to me anyway. My arms are covered in goosebumps and I rub them gently, trying to regain some warmth.

"Layton and I were more or less forced here because that idiot got an invitation from his ex." I raise my right eyebrow and look to Jasper, who raises his arms innocently and then smiles softly at me. I haven't seen Jadie at all today. If she invited him, where is she?

"Jadie's getting married tomorrow."

Oh. Who invites their ex-boyfriend to their wedding? It could hardly be more tactless. I'm assuming they didn't break up on good terms if Jasper ran off to New York to avoid seeing her.

He nervously kicks a small stone away and tilts his head. "I know it was probably more stupid than smart to accept the invitation. But I didn't want things to get awkward between us."

"Dude, I told you when you got the invitation that it was bullshit. Going there just makes everything more awkward."

"Maybe."

"I think it's an honorable decision, even if I could never do it. Facing my ex at his own wedding after so many years - that would probably be my nightmare," I interject and the boys look at me. My cheeks immediately flush and I want to look away, but I can't.

"I think the guy who would do that to you is the biggest asshole in the world." I giggle softly. "Then it's a good thing there are no candidates for that."

Valerian raises his eyebrows in surprise and I bite my tongue. I don't want them to think I'm a prude and still a little girl.

"No one at all?"

I shake my head.

"Because you're not in relationships or because there's just no man around?"

"I guess both?"

I'm not averse to having men over. But to build up feelings on a deep level only for the guy to end up cheating on me with my second cousin here in the village and breaking my heart? No, thank you. I can think of better things.

I'm not afraid of being touched. But I'm not someone who openly seeks it out either.

"Are there any women?" asks Valerian, and I shake my head again. "Are you crazy? I'd rather put a bullet in my head, you know how uptight people are here." He presses his lips together tightly and looks over at Jas, who returns his gaze briefly before looking away again. "So no women?" he asks again and I can't stop myself from pointing behind me at his bike. "You think that's what would have happened?"

Even if I can't explain it.

Or maybe I can.

He's simply irresistible.

"Don't you sometimes feel the need to have fun? To take someone and do what you want?" The look Valerian gives me is curious, perhaps even pleading. I weigh up inside whether I can risk following my impulsive decisions and just say something daring. To go for it.

Have a bit of fun.

Yeah... "You mean like making out with you on a motorcycle?"

His eyes widen a little, but I see them darken and he tightens. "Shit," he curses and grabs his crotch. I feel like I'm burning from the inside out.

"I don't think a woman like you should be driving home alone at this hour," Jasper interjects, licking his lips as his gaze moves from Valerian's crotch to me. My stomach turns upside down.

"I can take care of myself."

"Oh, I bet you can," Valerian growls and is about to pull out the pack of cigarettes again when I frown. "You really should stop smoking." He looks at me for a moment, a moment too long, and takes a deep breath. "Fuck, anything you want, little one," he says to me and then turns to Jasper, "does she make you that horny too?" Jasper doesn't answer him, but I can tell by the look on his face that he doesn't feel much different.

I decide to simply give in to an uncontrollable impulse and clear my throat briefly.

"You said you didn't have a place to stay yet. Maybe I have something for you."

3
The weekend deal

Marra

"It's really nice of you to let us sleep there." Jasper gives me a quick glance from his place behind the wheel.

In the side mirror, I can see the two motorcycles following us and I slide back and forth in my seat. I find out that Jasper has come to the restaurant in a cab, while Layton and Valerian have picked up their old Harley's from home.

After Layton joined us outside and I told the boys about my parents' cabin, which has been in the family since I was a kid, I offered to show them the way. I know the cabin by the lake is fully functional and ready to receive visitors, as my parents go there for the weekend from time to time. Two days in the woods, with a lake, a warm, cozy cabin and lots of alone time can never hurt.

I used to go there sometimes with my cousins when I was a kid, so the guest rooms should be functional.

"That's not a problem. There won't be anyone there anyway. I can give you the keys and you can just leave them under the doormat when you leave."

"That's really not a matter of course. You're really nice."

"You need to turn right here." He does as I tell him and we turn onto a secluded country road. We've been driving for twenty minutes and it's going to take a while, but I hope they can remember the way in the dark. "Do you still live in the white house with the blue roof? I remember seeing your father working outside the garage on Sundays."

I smile slightly at the memory of those times. He used to love tinkering with his old car or playing basketball with the hoop attached to the garage. As a child, he taught me how to shoot hoops and our summer days consisted of playing basketball for hours in front of the garage. Every now and then, kids from the neighborhood would join in.

"No. I moved further into the country. Even though I sometimes miss the dump," I say quietly. There was always something to repair at home.

"I miss it here sometimes too. But New York is great, you should check it out."

I turn down the music in the car a little. Jasper has chosen "Sex & Candy" by Marcy Playground. Interesting choice.

"No, that's not for me."

"Like relationships?"

I turn my head towards him and notice the cheeky grin on his lips. "It's not that I'm not interested in men. But you know how the species is from here." I grimace slightly at the thought of one or two of them.

No, definitely not.

I think I broke up with local men when my cousin's ex-boyfriend tried to make a pass at me.

"But we exist," he contradicts.

I swallow and rub my thighs.

"We were never like that."

Yes, that's true. Despite being born here, the three of them have never been as... strangely consumed and uptight as the others. At least that's how it seemed.

"We're *still* not like that," he corrects himself and heat shoots up my cheeks. I glance nervously over at him and he returns my gaze hard.

"What are you implying?" I ask.

"We're only here this weekend, Marra. If you want to experience something, this is your chance." My heart is almost beating out of my chest and his words tear my thoughts apart. I can see him swallowing hard too, but he doesn't take his eyes off me as he drives down the straight road.

"I mean, if you'd rather sleep in your own cabin than drive home alone at night, we're not going to force you out."

"I have a cat," I say quietly, completely overwhelmed, biting my lower lip.

"Surely your neighbors can look after him?" I don't tell him I don't have neighbors. I could text my mom.

What's the big deal?

God, just do it, Marra.

Just. Do. It.

But what will happen? Is it a stupid decision? Damn it.

"Where did you get that idea?" He laughs and runs his fingers through his tousled hair. "You just made out with Valerian like you've been waiting for it your whole life and like he's an oxygen tank you need to survive. Besides, you're sexy Marra. It would be a good deal for either of us."

"Why would I do that?" I ask, holding my breath. Getting an offer like this is insane. And it doesn't really suit me at all...

But he's right. They're only here for a weekend, and if I want to enjoy my time without regretting it, who else but them?

"Believe me, baby, you won't regret it. I want you to have some fun too. You've always held back before."

Because I feel comfortable in my warm nest.

But his words awaken a desire in me, a curiosity to find out more behind his words. I want to know what he wants me to do. I want to know what the boys can offer me. What he is inviting me to do.

I look deep into his warm, brown eyes and then nod curtly.

"I'll leave her a message. You're right, I shouldn't be out alone at night. I don't want to regret being so stupid and putting myself in danger."

He looks ahead again and I take a slow breath. I don't want him to realize how nervous I am. But it's so exciting.

And I love the adrenaline. Even though I've just moved further into the country for the peace and quiet, it can't hurt to have an adventure now and again.

I take out my old satellite phone, which I've saved up for for almost a year and a half, and leave a short message on my mother's machine.

"But do you think you'll regret it if you spend the night with us?"

His voice is calm and composed, but I bet he's just as anxious for my answer as I am.

"No."

Our eyes meet again.

"Pursuing your needs is something you should never regret."

"So you're going for it?"

I shrug my shoulders. "I think you need a distraction before you go to that wedding tomorrow. Valerian is in desperate need of a good mood and I doubt he'll have a problem with me staying there. And Layton," I say, but I don't know what to say about him. What reason would he have?

"Layton needs a weekend without consequences. His head is about to burst," he finishes the sentence for me.

"A weekend?"

"Our flight leaves on Sunday afternoon."

Should I stay with them for the whole weekend? My mother could take Leo with her, so that wouldn't be a problem. "And the wedding?"

"Be our plus one. I've already made plus one into plus two. Another third person won't stand out."

It's crazy, but just the thought of turning it down makes me think I'll be lying in my bed staring at the ceiling later. This offer is too tempting. And I would regret it if I didn't accept it.

I've always been attracted to all three of them, and having them all in my cabin in one fell swoop is like the fulfillment of my darkest dream. "How do you imagine it?"

"How do *you* imagine sex, Marra? Three men at once? Doing everything you crave with you? You tell me how you imagine it and I'll tell you - we'll give you more." The sensitive spot between my legs becomes warm again and pulsates. A soft moan escapes me and I press my thighs together. "Don't say that."

He takes one hand off the steering wheel and places it gently on my leg, which makes my heart beat even faster and makes me feel like I can barely breathe. The touch is electrifying - sends new life into my body.

Little lightning bolts make their tingling way across my skin and I lick my lips with excitement. It's been a long time since I've been touched the way Valerian and Jasper did in the last hour. And it didn't feel nearly as good then.

"Why not? I know you've already decided inside that you want us." I bite the inside of my cheeks. "Is that weird?"

He shakes his head and his hand slowly but surely moves further up my leg. "No, baby, that's human."

His fingers grip around the waistband of my pants and I let out a hissing breath.

Please keep talking to me. Tell me it's okay.

Please keep going.

Give me courage.

Do something.

And as if he could hear my thoughts, his hand slides into my pants and his fingers run over my most sensitive spot. I swallow, close my eyes for a moment and press my head against the headrest.

Oh my God.

"That's just the beginning, baby."

He strokes the fabric of my underpants and I'm instantly glad I'm wearing the good stuff today.

A tingle runs through my body, the desire for more grows and I want to squeeze my thighs even tighter against the sensation, but he pushes them apart and continues to play with the edge of my panties. I dig my fingers into the seat beneath me, open my eyes with flickering lids and notice the intense gaze with which he looks at me. Pure lust plays in his brown eyes and every now and then he casts a quick, scrutinizing glance ahead onto the road. We get closer and closer to the forest.

"You're so beautifully wet. I'd love to bury my face in your lap." His words trigger something in me, I don't know exactly what, but something inside me stirs and I press myself against his hand.

"Please," I gasp, and I'm not even sure what I'm asking him to do.

For him to make good on his words? For him to stop?

But as his fingers push the fabric aside and he strokes through my wetness, I stop thinking.

No thoughts. No regrets. No retreat.

Just this.

He caresses my pearl, and I moan out, wishing I could get out of this car and give myself to him completely

"Who would have thought that little Mar would crave my touch so much." I slide down a little as he pushes his fingers between my labia and penetrates even deeper, stroking me again and again, my wetness on his fingers.

"Have you thought about this before? When we were in class together?"

I don't really want to answer the question, maybe because I'm ashamed, maybe because my last sane thought wants to stop me from going any further. He had a girlfriend at the time. I shouldn't have wanted him in the first place.

"Tell me, baby."

"Fuck, yes," I gasp, and at the same moment, he inserts his fingers inside me. I bite my tongue to keep from moaning out loud again and press myself harder against the seat. That's too much. And too little at the same time. I don't want to stop. I need more.

"Yes, that's it."

He slides in and out, playing with my pearl again in between and my hands are now gripping the fabric of the seat so tightly that it hurts. The pulsation gets stronger and a wave builds up inside me that I don't want to let go of yet. I breathe harder and faster, but my throat is tight. His movements are so sure and practiced that I'm almost envious of every woman his fingers have touched before me. "You like that?"

I nod weakly and try to look at him, but I'm so blinded by the satisfaction and desire that I roll my eyes. "Talk to me."

"Yes," I say, "don't stop. I like it."

And he doesn't stop. A heat rolls over me and I get closer and closer to my orgasm. Moaning, I blink a few times.

"I want to stay with you. The whole fucking weekend. I want you to fuck me." His fingers speed up, but he doesn't rub too hard and the tension falls away from me more and more.

Suddenly he grabs my chin and pulls me towards him. Stormily, he puts his lips on mine and licks mine with his tongue, our teeth bumping against each other as his fingers bring me closer and closer to climax.

I moan into his mouth, he bites my lip gently - and then he pulls away from me. I'm only five seconds away from cumming when he pulls his fingers out of me too and leans back. Only now do I realize that we've stopped and are no longer on the street.

In front of us is my parents' hut. "I want you to ride my cock and cum on my mouth. But not here in the car, baby. Let's go inside." My rapidly pounding heart and shortness of breath prevent me from saying anything, so I look around hesitantly and recognize the two other men in the dark who have pulled up next to us on their motorcycles. They look at us in the car, and when they notice my gaze, Valerian tilts his head with a grin and Layton runs a hand over his short hair.

Jasper gets out, walks around my car and opens the door for me. "Get out and let yourself in for a weekend full of passion and lust. A weekend where anything can happen. With no consequences, no regrets and no future. Let us spoil you, baby."

4
Raised weapons and a lot of patience

Marra

I unlock the front door with trembling fingers and smile wryly as the woody scent wafts towards me. The men are hot on my heels. I flick the light switch and step further into the living room to give them more space. We are all alone.

"That's it."

The living room consists of a large couch, next to which is an old wicker basket with plaid wool blankets and cushions, a small table, a fireplace and a tube TV. The adjoining kitchen is not particularly large, but it was always big enough to feed my hungry cousins and me. At the end of the room, a staircase leads up to the second floor, where there are five bedrooms with balconies and a bathroom.

"Doesn't look bad," I hear Layton say, and watch as the boys carry in their three bags, which I've stowed in the back of my truck. The heat is still prickling under my skin, and I lean against the wall at my back for support.

How far can I go?

What am I capable of?

"Just make yourself comfortable," I say and scurry up the stairs. When I get to the bathroom, I close the door behind me and take a deep breath. This is madness.

I run water over my hands and take a closer look at my reflection. I don't look too bad. My hair is a little tousled from the friction of the headrest, but not so much that I look like a scarecrow. My lips are swollen and a little red because I've bitten them hard several times. My cheeks are also glowing pink and my eyes are shiny. My make-up has faded. Sighing, I splash a little water on my face, take a deep breath and leave the bathroom again.

As I step into the dark corridor, my gaze falls on Valerian, who is leaning against the wall with his arms crossed and looking at me mildly.

I give him a shy smile and he makes a curt movement of his head to tell me to come to him.

I stay close to him as he rubs a strand of my hair between his fingers and looks down at my lips.

I don't know why his presence has such an intense effect on me, but I can't help but enjoy it.

That's why I'm here, isn't it? To get the attention of three such attractive men and melt under it, to spend the nights with them - that's the whole point of this arrangement.

"Did you enjoy feeling Jas's fingers inside you?" His rough voice gives me goosebumps again and the hairs on the back of my neck stand up. So he's seen exactly what we've been up to. Maybe that should bother me if I had a normal, healthy mind. But apparently that's not the case, because it has the opposite effect on me. Valerian has been watching us, even Layton might have seen it, and it turns me the hell on.

I lean toward him, my lips close to the shell of his ear. "He didn't let me come," I whisper, noticing the smile that creeps onto his lips.

He pulls me towards him with one hand and I notice he's holding something with the other. I take a quick look down and shudder. He is holding my father's hunting rifle, which must have been leaning against the wall earlier. I look him uncertainly in the eye again and he raises the rifle provocatively. Overwhelmed, I back away and watch in horror as he presses the barrel against my chest.

I open my lips to protest, but he beats me to it.

"I wanted to fuck you when I was eighteen, and seven fucking years later, you still get under my skin so much that I wish I could have fucked you on the restaurant table in front of everyone."

I swallow hard.

How come he never spoke to me back then? Never really talked to me?

He was like a silent observer, a few wicked and deep looks, a smile when we were close, but never more.

My heart is running a marathon.

He presses the gun harder against my chest, making me stagger backwards and bump into the wall.

He takes a step towards me. Should I make a confession too?

The wicked grin on his face tells me that I should.

So I take a deep breath and try to support him in his confession.

"I imagined being fucked by you when I was eighteen years old, and the image has never faded." A storm breaks loose in his eyes, next to which an EF 5 tornado looks harmless. I like what my words trigger in him, and without further ado, he tosses the gun aside and is with me, his breath brushing my skin, and I catch just a glimpse of his lips before he presses them to mine. For the second time that evening, I weaken in his arms and wrap my hands around his neck.

The kiss is intense, engaging and breathtaking.

"You're so damn sexy," he gasps and licks his tongue over my lips. His fingers claw into my ass and he lifts me up. I wrap my legs around his torso and lean further down towards him. He deepens the kiss, catches me with a moan and presses me firmly against the wall. I'm still totally exhilarated from the car ride and happiness hormones are flooding through me, the pulsing of my pussy is getting stronger, almost painful. "I need more," I say and he growls excitedly. I can feel how hard he is.

A thick bulge presses against my sensitive center. Eighteen-year-old me wouldn't believe a word of what's happening.

Valerian King and I are making out. Jasper Bailey fingering me in my car.

Layton Reed is sitting in my living room, probably waiting for me.

Fucking hell, shoot me.

Valerian wants it as much as I do, and this gives me the validation I've always dreamed of.

I'm back on the floor in a flash, and he unzips my shorts with nimble fingers, they slide down my legs and land on the floor, Valerian has easy access and pulls at my panties too. Cold night air brushes my legs, which must be coming in through an open window, and I shiver slightly. Which must be due not only to the cold, but also to the tingling desire and pure lust. I open his suit trousers and see the large bulge behind his boxer shorts. Excited, I bite my lower lip and gently stroke the thin fabric. He watches me, one hand leaning against the wall next to my head and a wry grin on his face. I push it down and his plump, stiff cock jumps out at me.

He's damn sexy.

I feel like I'm dreaming and never want to wake up again.

The wetness must be gradually running down my thighs.

"Lift your leg, starlet," he says, and I do as he says. He grabs it securely and firmly, wraps it around his waist and presses me tighter between him and the wall. Now that my legs are spread, revealing my naked midriff, he licks his lips eagerly. With his other hand, he grabs his cock and thrusts his hips towards me. I stare unblinking into his eyes as he rubs the tip of his cock against my labia. The tingling intensifies and I let out a breathless moan. It's as if someone is tickling me and stroking me gently at the same time. My fingers claw into his white shirt and he continues to slowly rub through my wetness. Again and again, he moves from my pearl to my entrance and back again.

I want to explode.

Our short breathing is the only thing I hear, his lust and horniness is the only thing I see. "Valerian," I whisper greedily and he presses his tip against my entrance a little more, but doesn't push all the way in. I want to stretch out towards him, hoping he'll finally penetrate, but he holds me back and stays just an inch inside me.

"I love the way you say my name," he whispers against my ear and penetrates another inch. It's not enough. My feet cramp in my boots and I cling to him even tighter.

"God, please Valerian, deeper." But he prefers to play some more, pulling out the little bit I was allowed to taste and rubbing his cock up and down between my wetness again.

"Patience, little Mar. You'll get what you crave."

I can't take it anymore. "My good girl."

5
Tequila around 0 o'clock

Layton

asper and I push our bags to the edge of the room, and out of the corner of my eye I see Valerian following Marra up the stairs. My fingers and toes are tingling to do the same and follow her, but I don't want to steal her privacy.

I've become a pro when it comes to not crossing the line between me and her. I've always held back and put her need for peace and quiet above my own. I did this not only because I respect her, but because we were really good friends and she is still important to me in some ways. Even after years of no contact, our connection hasn't lost its importance and I would rather shoot myself than let her suffer through me.

It's always been like that between us.

It used to be adolescent feelings, butterflies in the stomach and falling in love in phases. But Marra was always just there - and never more.

"I can't believe I'm seeing her again after so many years," I mumble to myself and Jasper looks over at me. He puts chopped wood in the fireplace. Although it's summer, it's starting to get colder, it's pitch dark outside and a little fire won't do us any harm.

"She lives here," he remarks and I put my hands on my hips.

"I realize that, you smartass. But who would have thought we'd actually see her again? Or that the evening would end like this?"

Jas lets the wood burst into flames. "Marra was always good for a surprise."

I frown at his words and wonder what he means. Because Marra hates surprises. She's the kind of girl who deliberately lets books and movies tell her the ending.

She's never been the kind of girl who plays games or makes reckless decisions. You can usually predict her next move, and that's why I enjoyed spending time with her.

When she's around, all the hustle and bustle takes a break. The noise in my ears disappears. The screams in my head fall silent.

I felt safe and secure with her because I knew where I stood. Because she's predictable, the kind of person who doesn't step out of line and attack me unexpectedly from behind.

You could get used to her.

"You saw her as the standout girl, Lay." The left corner of his mouth lifts and his gaze goes distant as he sits down on the armchair in front of the fireplace. He seems to be thinking about the old memory. "When we were younger, she told me that she sometimes liked to escape." There is a brief silence and the fire devours the wood with a crackling sound. "She wasn't unhappy, you know that better than anyone. But she wanted to know what it felt like to be unpredictable for a change."

He lifts his gaze from the flames.

I laugh with a snort.

That's bullshit.

"But that's what gives her comfort. She's been going to this reunion for seven years, every damn September. And afterwards, she always sits in the same spot in the bar and drinks tequila." I can't hold back my words in time.

Jasper doesn't miss it either, of course. "How do you know that?"

"I still have my contacts here, even though we've moved away, Jas. Contacts who keep me up to date and inform me about everything. I know Marra still ticks the same way she did back then. Habit is her shell, her protective mechanism."

He shrugs and pokes at the fire with a metal rod. "That's exactly it. She probably wanted to see if she could do it. If she can break out of herself and the cage she's built around herself without the world collapsing around her. She never went through with it, she made a conscious decision to live in peace. But the urge and curiosity for something else may still be there, Lay."

I sit down too, resting my forearms on my knees. In my head, one piece of the puzzle fits into another.

"This is her outburst, isn't it? The one she told you about as a teenager. No rules, no expectations. Nothing she could see out for herself."

Jas nods. "I guess so. We're the perfect guinea pigs."

"She's always been interested in us." "That's why I made her this offer and I don't seem to be completely wrong in my assessment, as she quickly agreed."

I let this realization sink in for a moment and run my hand over my face. Marra is an amazing woman.

She's sexy and smart. Brave and reserved at the same time. I've never seen her like this before, and that's probably her goal. She wants to test herself.

Suddenly Jasper laughs dryly and shakes his head. Then his expression becomes serious again. "What do we do if she wants more after this weekend? Or, even worse, if she gets addicted to the adrenaline of testing herself? If she wants more chaos?"

There is a rustling outside the hut, perhaps a deer or a rabbit that has come a little too close. "That's not our problem then, Jas. You set the rules with her."

He raises an eyebrow. "And what if it does become our problem?"

I have no answer to that and stare silently into his faithful brown eyes before rising with a sigh.

It's not something I'm going to worry about now. Because it won't come to that. Marra wants to try things out. To experience a few things. But she's not stupid, she knows there's no future in this. Not for a long time. It's long since too late for this path.

"Let's go and see what they've been up to for so long."

He peers into the blazing flames once more, then follows me. When I reach the first step of the stairs, he puts a hand on my shoulder and I give him a cursory glance.

"Let's just make sure we can all enjoy this weekend. Without consequences."

I nod.

That's exactly what I'm going to do. I've been just her silent and trusted friend for long enough.

Now it's time to show her what else I can be.

The closer we get to the foot of the stairs, the louder the stifled moans and muffled voices of Val and Marra become. I swallow deeply and frown.

Jasper is also getting restless as we stop in front of the last step of the stairs and watch the spectacle unfolding before us.

My cock is getting hard and wants out of my pants as I watch my best friend and old girlfriend fuck. Valerian holds her pressed against the wall and rubs his cock against her, pushing her to the limit.

I can feel Jasper's heavy breathing on the back of my neck and I suspect he's getting as hard and stiff as I am.

This girl has always been perfection.

Her plump tits, which are not too big and not too small, are almost slipping out of her yellow top, but she's so distracted by Valerian that she doesn't notice.

Marra has always been dirty, she just never let on. But when we were still close friends, I learned what she's like. She has her needs, she just never acted on them. It was only a matter of time before she exploded and took the full dose. I never expected to be there, but I'm glad I talked to her tonight. Just showing up here for this stupid wedding. But deep down, I was hoping to see her again.

I always had a bit of a soft spot for her. I knew she found me attractive, appealing. But she never made a move and out of respect I held back.

But now it's different. We're more mature, more reckless. I like that she takes what she wants.

And she wants us.

My cock twitches behind my zipper.

"This is so fucking awesome," I hear Jas whisper softly and I nod absently. "She's always been perfect, Jas. If only you knew what she was like in private."

She was dancing in front of me, she's a damn good dancer, taking the joint between her lips like she was afraid of crushing it. She lay with her head on my chest and slept while I did everything I could not to get hard and fall all over her. If our old friends hadn't been there, I wouldn't have been able to promise anything.

How she used to come into the little bar where I worked at the weekend with friends just to talk to me and smile at me. She always had this special smile when she looked at me. And when we went out to eat and she didn't have any money to get anything, I always left her some of my food and pretended I was full so she could eat my leftovers.

Marra was always there. In the back of my mind. She was a secret crush, a girl who was too perfect to be true, a good friend. And it stayed with the latter.

I step out of our dark, safe hiding place and clear my throat.

If Valerian fucks her, it will be in front of us. With us.

Once again, I don't let her slip through my fingers.

Her eyes look at me in panic, but she no longer seems ashamed of having been caught. I walk towards her and Valerian takes a step back, nodding confidently at me. The three of us have grown together like brothers over the years. Nothing works without these idiots.

"You don't fuck a woman like her against a wall in the dark. Let's show her what it means to be desired and fully satisfied." I grab her hand and pull her out of her daze behind me, down the stairs into the well-lit living room.

A warm atmosphere surrounds the room, and that's a good thing.

I don't want Marra to feel uncomfortable between us. I want her to enjoy.

She sinks gently onto the couch, and I reach for a blanket to place under her neck and hips. Valerian and Jas enter the room behind us as I pull the top over her head. Her breasts are exposed and I bend over them, kissing each nipple and biting gently. Then I spread kisses over her skin, from her breasts to her collarbone to the sensitive spot under her ear. Once there, I lower my voice so that only she can hear me. "You've always asked me who the girl is that would always have a chance with me, but I've never given you an answer."

I lift my gaze and look into her soft brown eyes. They shine hopefully and I'm glad to be able to give her the answer she wants to hear.

"It's always been you, Marra. Ever since I met you when I was fourteen."

I continue kissing her across her jaw until I graze her lips. My cock is now pulsing so painfully with desire that I wish I could plunge myself into her right now. I've waited far too long for this moment. She runs her fingers over my tense arms and her nipples erect. "I've wanted to do this to you for a long time."

"Then it's high time," she replies and I kiss her deeply. Our lips meet brutally and I run a hand along her body. Her soft curves feel perfect under my fingers.

How long I have dreamed of this moment. Touching her like this feels like a gift, as if I've been given a sacred power that was never meant for me. And yet I have it now.

I detach myself from her and run another hand over her breasts before lowering myself between her thighs and licking along them. Out of the corner of my eye, I see Jas and Valerian coming towards me. Valerian is now completely naked too and Jas pulls his shirt over his head.

This is going to be one hell of an exciting weekend.

6

Piercings and forbidden honey

Marra

think I'm dead. It can't be anything else.

This must be the reward for all the years I've kept a low profile and always been nice and kind. For the trust I've put in peace and tranquillity. It feels like a gift from heaven.

Layton slips his head between my legs and licks his tongue along the inside of my thigh. This touch alone is almost too much. My heart is racing and my body is in a state of total ecstasy. I lean my head back with pleasure and press it into the pillow Lay has laid me on.

I don't think anymore. I've long since jumped off the cliff of sanity. I've given up control.

And I don't want it back.

My gaze falls on Jasper, who has sat down next to me and is looking down at me. The expression in his eyes is wild, almost torn.

My pulse quickens at the sight of him, his jeans hanging open and loose to his knees, his shirt up a little so I can catch a glimpse of his abs.

I swallow hard and claw my hands into the fabric of the couch as Lay's tongue continues to circle and trace lines over my skin. Grinning, I bite my lower lip and keep eye contact with Jasper.

My mind is foggy with happiness.

"Feeling good, baby?" I nod slightly and he starts to smile, his tousled brown hair giving him an air of gentleness.

"What about you?" I ask, his excitement growing.

"First, we're going to take care of you." He leans down to me, presses his lips to mine and puts a hand to my cheek. His tenderness robs me of my last breath and I want to pounce on him immediately.

His tongue, which is still driving me crazy, slides between my labia and Layton licks over my wetness. I whimper and slide a little deeper, forcing my mouth to pull away from Jasper.

Suddenly, I feel his fingers gently stroking my skin, sliding between my breasts and making my body tingle. I flinch under the touch because it feels too tempting, and with butterflies in my stomach, I want to tear myself away from his touch because I feel like I can barely breathe. But I stay where I am and watch as two men touch me at the same time and I burst into flames inside.

Layton grabs my thighs firmly and pushes them further apart. I just let him do it without a word. He makes me feel like he knows what he's doing.

And it feels sinfully good.

Shit.

Suddenly he pulls back, grabs me by the hips and turns me onto all fours. I gasp, startled, and look up at Jasper, who's looking at me like he wants to devour me. I swallow hard.

Maybe it's all too much.

Too much at once.

I'm not used to this kind of touch and suddenly question my decision to have agreed to this deal.

Jas puts a hand on my cheek, caresses my skin and lets it move to my neck, where he squeezes tightly. I whimper under his firm grip and close my eyes for a moment. At the same time, Layton opens my legs a little and I feel his tongue at my entrance again. This time from behind, more intense - more dominant. He licks between my cleft, sucks up all my doubts and lets me fall.

Falling.

Deep, deep, deep.

And I don't hit the floor with a dull thud.

No, I continue to float.

He digs his fingers into my ass and starts kneading it, which distracts me for a second so that I almost completely forget Jasper, who has taken off his underpants and is standing naked in front of me. I lick my lips hungrily at the sight of him. His body is muscular, but not too much so and he has quite narrow hips, which only makes his penis look even bigger.

And damn, it's big.

And he's pierced.

Holy shit.

He grabs me by the hair and pushes my head back a little as I struggle not to sink even lower onto Layton's face. I greedily take Jasper into my mouth, licking over his pierced tip and along his shaft until I have him almost all the way in my mouth. Slowly, I start to move my head back and forth and I look up at him, looking for confirmation that I'm doing everything right.

And although he looks at me intently, as if he can't feel anything I'm doing, I can see it. His left eye twitches for a split second and he swallows hard. The grip in my hair tightens and I whimper as Lay slides one finger inside me, widening me, and then adds a second. "Fuck, baby, you're doing good," I hear Jasper say, and if I wasn't so distracted, I'm sure I'd be blushing. But there's no time for that, because as I continue to suck Jasper off and Layton licks and fingers my pearl, my eyes fall on Valerian.

He's standing naked next to the couch, watching us.

Me.

His gaze is strange, almost frightening.

Then I discover the small tattoo on his hip - a brush whose hair paints a fine line that leads into the cable of headphones. Just the sight of it sends the same wave through me that I felt in the car.

I want to scream with pleasure.

But I lick over Jasper's shaft and tense my legs as Layton hits a sensitive spot and I melt into an orgasm beneath him - my eyes still locked on Valerian.

"You taste like sweet, forbidden honey," Lay grumbles softly as he simply licks up my orgasm and then stands up behind me. Valerian approaches us and I pull away from Jasper, who lets go of my hair but doesn't miss the opportunity to stroke my cheek again. "I don't know what to say," I admit, but Jas just shrugs. "Don't say anything, baby. Feel."

Valerian is with me, traveling over my curves and pulling me away from Jasper-closer to him and merging our lips together. His cock touches my stomach and I immediately feel a kind of pleasure again that I've rarely felt before.

How can you be so charged with feelings and sensations in just a few minutes? I feel high, like I'm on a fucking trip.

He runs his fingertips over my shoulders, over the bare skin of my arms, causing goose bumps to spread all over my body. When he pulls away from me, he looks deeply at me with the blue eyes I've always raved about and bites down hard on my lower lip.

A sharp pain jolts through my body and I taste the metallic blood, but he licks it away, turns us together on the couch so he's under me and then gently sits me down on his stiff cock. I lean my head back and moan loudly - because, damn it, it feels like he's impaling me from the inside.

I'm so horny I'm afraid I'm going to dribble all over him, but as I slowly start to ride him, moving my hips in a rhythmic beat on top of him, it suddenly feels so easy.

Like I've never done anything else before.

Straining and breathing heavily, I touch the tattoo and he flinches slightly.

I know what it means.

Has he told his boys?

Starlet, it echoes through my head and I realize that I completely missed the nickname earlier. He called me starlet.

My throat tightens.

He seems to realize what I'm thinking about and thrusts his hips into my ride and I groan. He follows my every move with his eyes.

"Do you remember that day, little Mar?"

I lower my upper body onto his, chest to chest, and my lips hover close over his.

It's the first time I've ever been this intimate with a man.

And then it's several men and not just one.

I must be an all-or-nothing girl.

The tingling between my legs doesn't subside, on the contrary, I have the feeling that it's only getting stronger. "How could I ever forget?" I whisper close to his ear and he bites the crook of my neck in agreement. Grinning, I straighten up again and continue the ride, my ego soaring into the clouds.

He got a tattoo for me. And I thought he'd never really noticed me.

He runs his hands up and down my curves before holding me close and matching my movements, moving his hips against me in rhythm. I lean my head back, moan and feel myself breaking open inside. My pussy tightens around his cock and I have to dig my fingers into his skin to keep from crying out loud.

It feels so criminally good, it should be illegal.

Suddenly Jasper is behind me, and I feel him rubbing something wet between my ass - it must be his spit, and I try to look at him over my shoulder, meeting his soft eyes and mischievous grin. He licks his lips greedily and runs a closed fist over his shaft before leaning down towards me and seeking the entrance to my anus with the tip. I slow down my movements, my heart beating far too fast, and wait for the feeling of having two cocks inside me at the same time. I swallow and let it happen with my eyes closed. Growling, but still with feeling, Jas makes his way inside me and I gasp for air. It doesn't feel quite as painful as I thought it would, but it's a strange sensation.

Almost as if I'm whole and not half.

Somehow powerful and like the men are giving me something I've always needed. Jasper's piercing rubs coolly against my skin, making it pulse painfully, and I'm on the verge of cumming again. Valerian taps my thigh with two fingers after watching us carefully. I move again and Jasper waits a moment before increasing the pace and then thrusting rhythmically into me.

It's gigantic.

This moment... robs me of every breath, every thought of anything bad, and any chance of regretting this.

"You're doing so fucking good, baby," Jas says roughly, thrusting even deeper into me. I fall a little onto Valerian, who grins and holds me by the shoulders. I'm barely able to move under my own power, which is why Valerian takes over my part and moves independently from underneath me.

Tears gather in my eyes because I am so overwhelmed that I feel like crying. When I blink a few times, I recognize Layton in front of me, who has positioned himself above Valerian. His bulging cock sticks out at me and I reach for it, running my hand up and down until I can't hold on any longer and have to brace myself again. Instead, I lick over the tip and shaft with my tongue, take it all in my mouth and continue to play with his skin with my tongue. When I let it slide out again, he reaches into my hair and waits briefly until I've caught my breath, then he pushes himself towards me and I let my retracted lips move up and down.

At the same time, Valerian takes a hand from my shoulder and guides it down to my pearl, where he begins to play with it, rubbing and tweaking it. I moan around Lay's cock and Jasper moans deeply too as he realizes how aroused I am at this moment.

Damn.

"She's so fucking perfect," I hear Valerian say indistinctly and Jasper slaps my ass, but I don't flinch.

Quite the opposite.

It makes me even wetter and my pussy must be dripping by now. My stomach muscles tense and relax every time one of the boys hits a deep spot or makes me come. I don't know how much time has passed, but it must be hours of them changing positions, just licking or fingering me and letting me relax before splitting me again, tearing me apart and patching me back up. My screams, our moans and their growls sound like a continuous loop in my ears, bouncing off the wooden wall like an echo and arousing me even more.

Hours of Jasper caressing my skin and gently slapping me as if it were one and the same.

Hours in which Valerian looks at me so closely it's as if he's devouring me and whispers things in my ear again and again.

Hours in which Layton takes me from every conceivable position as if there were no tomorrow.

Tomorrow...

What will happen when they return to the airport? Then there will be no tomorrow.

"What are you thinking about, little Mar?" I have my head pressed down on a pillow - my arms have long since lost the strength to hold me up. My butt is stretched up in the air and Layton is thrusting hard into me. My voice is raspy and feels scratchy as I come shakily, screaming for the hundredth time that night and Lay cums on my back too. I sink into myself on the couch and immediately feel Jasper bed me on his lap and brush my sweaty hair out of my face. "I'm happy," I whisper in response and he laughs softly. "This is what we wanted."

And I really mean it.

There is a warm and unfamiliar feeling in my chest that has kept me from letting myself fall powerless for hours. These men have given me the opportunity to do something I was never prepared for myself. And I really like that.

Valerian stands at the open window, still naked and his eyes on me, but he blows the smoke from his cigarette out the window into the rain pattering on the porch outside.

I don't tease him and let him smoke, after all, he's been holding back for me for many hours.

And concentrates on completely different things.

"Thank you," I say, before my tired eyelids slowly close and everything goes black.

7

Blanket fight and Italian love poems

Marra

I wake up to the icy cold touching my legs. I protectively pull them towards me and stay in a kind of fetal position, but I don't get any warmer.

Gritting my teeth, I grope in the darkness for something soft and, above all, warm. When my fingers come across something hard and quite obviously alive, because the reaction to my wild poking around is a deep grumbling, I reluctantly open my eyes and look in the direction from which the deep noises are coming.

"Give it back!" I whisper in a raspy voice so as not to wake the others. Valerian frowns and clings to the blanket like a koala to its tree. Sighing, I reach for his fingers and want to release them as gently as possible from the tight grip, but I pause for a moment and take a closer look at him.

He looks kinda of cute.

When he's asleep and clinging to something like that damn blanket, he doesn't look like the evil biker businessman from New York, he looks like a little boy who desperately needed to sleep. His light blond hair is tousled and his full lips are slightly parted. His chest rises and falls evenly.

He looks like a more striking and tougher version of Boyd Holbrook. With his stubbly beard and highlights hanging in his face, he reflects a certain intensity that I haven't seen from him before.

I'm about to sit up and look for another blanket to let the poor guy sleep when I notice the slight twitch in the corner of his right mouth. Furious, I stay in my position and take a closer look.

There it is again: a twitch, as if he is stifling a laugh.

Without another moment's hesitation, I slap him on the shoulder and grab the last corner of the blanket still peeking out of his folded arms and give it a good tug. "It's mine," he grumbles, but I don't let him stop me and keep pulling. "Val, I'm cold."

That's enough now. I grab the blanket with both hands and tug at it as if my life depends on the last corner of it. But Val just grumbles, turns around ... and pulls me with him.

"Ah!"

With a whump, I land half on top of him, and his elbow digs painfully into my stomach. My knee bumps into his ribs, his hand is - of course - on my thigh and his lips are far too close to my neck.

"You can just tell me that this is your favorite way to wake up. Then we can do it like this every day now, starlet." His voice is raspy and I sigh deeply. "You stole my blanket!"

He doesn't answer me again, is frighteningly quiet and his chest rises in slow, gentle movements. Did he really fall back asleep so quickly?

"At least share it with me," I try, but he doesn't even bother to make a small sound. I slide off him, which must look like a seal struggling to land, and then kick his legs with my feet.

Jasper is lying on the other side of the sofa - a really good decision by my parents to buy a sofa bed where about six people can lie stretched out next to each other, if you have the motivation to squeeze in between that many people. But I can't see anything of Layton for miles around.

"Valerian," I whisper and pull his hair, but his head only follows my movement. Sighing, I rub my arms. It's not just about the cold anymore - it's a power struggle.

Because I know that Valerian knows exactly what's going on here.

My God - he even laughed at me.

"Well, I'm off to the bedroom to sleep." I want to get up from the couch, even reach for the backrest to pull myself up, but then I hear a grumble behind me. I turn to him and see that he has one arm outstretched towards me.

His eyes are still closed and there is a blissful calm on his tired face.

Because he's not expecting it, I reach for the blanket in a flash and pull it away from him. Startled, he opens his pretty little eyes and looks at me, stunned. "Well done, Marra, now we're both cold."

I roll my eyes and crawl over to him, sit on his hip and press his shoulders onto the couch.

A wicked smile forms on my lips.

"Tough luck, blanket thief. You could have just given it back to me, then we'd both still be warm."

"But I wanted to tease you."

"Then you know who's the guilty party here."

He grins and grabs my thighs, squeezes them tightly and lets his gaze glide along my naked body. There's a rustling beside us and I notice Jasper lift his head from the pillows with a dreamy look on his face. At first he doesn't quite seem to realize what's happening, but then he lets his head fall back with a sigh and lets his neck crack.

He looks at us with a grin and then rests his head on one arm, amused. "Didn't think you'd be *that* dominant, Marra."

He points at us with his free hand and I slide off Valerian with flushed cheeks, grabbing the blanket I threw behind us earlier and wrapping it around my body.

"Oh starlet, you don't need to hide."

I sit upright at the head of the couch and lean against the cushion. "You have no right to talk to me anymore. I don't talk to thieves." He laughs and leans forward to take a strand of my hair between his fingers and wind it. I stare down at him in silence, watching his body tense and relax again. His blue eyes are fixed on me the whole time and I want to melt under his gaze.

"I'm much worse than a thief, Marra."

I frown in surprise. "What do you mean?"

He just shrugs.

Jasper looks at him for a few seconds with a dangerous gleam in his eye, then turns to me with an affectionate smile. "Don't listen to him. He likes to talk crap at night that isn't true."

He gets up from the couch, also still naked, and I watch him with my lips pressed together. Only when his tight butt disappears behind the kitchen island do I look at Valerian again.

He raises an eyebrow provocatively, whereupon I snort and give him the middle finger.

Fuck him.

Jasper opens a few wall cupboards, then seems to have found what he was looking for and turns to us triumphantly. "How about a little drinking game? Val wake Lay up."

Groaning, Valerian rolls over the couch like he's six years old. "That guy's a grouch when you wake him up at night."

I giggle and Val pushes himself up, stretches and disappears into the hallway.

I get up from the couch as well, grab some clothes to dress myself and Jas, and walk over to him, grabbing four glasses from the cupboard. I take the bottle of whisky and start to fill the glasses. I walk up to Jasper, who grins and gives me a hug. He's so tall that he can rest his chin on my head. I snuggle against his warm chest and close my eyes. His shirt smells like a mixture of lemons and cigarettes, but somehow it's pleasant.

"Why doesn't Lay sleep with us?"

He leans down to my ear and gently bites the crook of my neck before whispering, "He prefers to sleep alone, baby. That's just the way he is, the way he's most comfortable."

He leans back and I look into his deep brown eyes. I don't need to know the reasons to understand, but I can just accept it. "Just wait until Valerian realizes I stole his clothes, then Layton will thank me for waking him up for this laughing matter."

The corners of Jasper's mouth twitch and I point to the floor behind the kitchen island, where I quickly tossed Valerian's clothes after my escape to Jasper.

He shakes his head in satisfaction and strokes my hair and forehead. "You're messing with the devil."

"He's pretty sweet to me."

"I wouldn't call his bluff, baby."

Smirking, I take two glasses and place them on the living room table while Jasper spins the whiskey bottle. "This isn't going to end well," he whispers, looking into the hallway where Val has disappeared. "If he manages to get Lay out of bed," he says, and not a second later I hear a muffled thump, followed by an angry curse.

"WHAT THE HELL?!" Layton's grumpy voice echoes through the cabin. Jasper and I look at each other, waiting - then we burst out laughing.

"Bloody hell, Valerian!" Then a hard thud.

"Did he kill him?" I gasp between laughs and Jas shakes his head. "Either Valerian pushed him out of bed or shoved the pillow in his face."

"Or both," I add, whereupon Jasper takes a swig from the bottle.

A minute later, Val struts into the living room, smug as a king who's just been crowned - with a disheveled, visibly bad-tempered Layton in tow.

"That was an assassination attempt," growls Lay, his hair sticking out in all directions. "I could have died."

Valerian raises his index finger in correction and stretches his back. "That was an effective wake-up call, my friend. It's the kind of thing you learn early on when you're friends with someone like you."

I shake my head with a laugh and play with the glass in my hands.

Valerian turns in a circle with a confident grin, surveys the room and licks his lips. "Now sit down and drink with us. I let you get away alive, that's reason enough to celebrate." Layton rolls his eyes and sits down in front of the fireplace. But I continue to watch the naked Valerian, whose grin is now slipping from his lips and who is still looking around in irritation.

Oh, how good it feels to see him so confused for once, even if he still stands in the room with his proud and well-trained body as if he were Adonis.

"Stop teasing him, Marra," Jasper hisses, and I stick my tongue out at him. "Shut the fuck up. It's about the blanket, I'm not joking around here." I lean back on the couch and listen as Valerian continues to trudge through the living room, wondering aloud in frustration, "Where's my stuff?" I can't help but laugh out loud.

"I've hidden them," I admit and immediately feel his penetrating gaze on me. "What?" His voice immediately gets sharper, but I don't let on. I point to the kitchen island and he makes his way there, snorting.

"You're the fucking devil," he growls, and I give Jasper a triumphant look. "See? I'm not messing with the devil. More like a little kid - I'm the devil here."

I speak louder to Valerian: "What did you expect? You started the fight with the blanket."

Layton grumbles something ironic to himself, puts the wood in the fireplace and gets it burning again. "Come here now, Val, and get dressed already."

Valerian gets dressed, but winks playfully at Jasper. "Come on, I can see you're enjoying the show, buddy." He wants to argue with Val again, but I quickly intervene and hand them both a glass of whisky.

Jasper moves a little closer too.

"Come on then, little Mar." Layton looks at me, waiting.

I pretend to think for a moment and stare at the rim of my glass. Then I smile diabolically and Val leans forward, propping himself up on his legs.

"How many of you have ever hurt yourselves during sex?" After I ask the question, I put on my best poker face.

Silence.

Then Jasper clears his throat and Layton grins, probably knowing what Jas is about to say, and his bad mood seems to be forgotten. "Does it count if I accidentally fell off the bed?"

I laugh out loud. "Oh my God."

"It was a bunk bed," Layton adds, and Jasper gives him a venomous look. Valerian snorts. "A BUNK BED?!"

Jasper rolls his eyes in embarrassment and rubs his thighs. "That was just after we moved to New York. I was trying to take my mind off the breakup, and Layton dragged me to a cheap bar where a 17-year-old girl was pretending to be 19, but I was so drunk I didn't realize I'd walked into her childhood bedroom with a bunk bed. In the end, I didn't even care - until I fell." Valerian pats me on the shoulder, laughing, and I join in. And I thought all embarrassing stories came from him or Layton, but not Jasper.

"Tell me more," Layton begins, grinning cynically and leaning backwards, relaxed. "How deep was the fall? Did it really hurt?"

"How painful would you call it if two weeks later I was still walking around like a penguin? You asshole know exactly how the story goes."

"Yeah, but it's funny to hear. Even the third time."

"What about you?" I turn to Val because I want to know if he has an embarrassing story to tell too. But he just shrugs his shoulders and takes a sip. "I remain a mystery."

"Coward," I tease him and he taps the tip of my nose.

"I think it's only fair if I tell one of the most embarrassing booze stories about our revered Valerian in return, but be careful, it's relatively long." I nod at Jasper in agreement and ask him to continue. Valerian, who has just raised his glass to his lips, pauses dangerously. "Dare, Jasper Bailey, and these will be the last breaths you ever tell a story with."

Layton rolls his eyes with a sigh and slaps his hands over his face. "Not this arguing again."

Valerian looks at him and laughs out loud. I look back and forth between the two of them tensely, my heart beating rapidly against my chest - because this moment makes me incredibly happy.

I am happy.

So, so happy I could scream.

"Usually most of the shit we've done is Layton's fault, Marra, so he can't really complain," Jasper says, and Layton raises his hands innocently. "I'm always a good chaperone."

"Yeah, until you suddenly disappear because you find something else more interesting. Usually it's an XX chromosome on two legs, with long, beautiful hair, preferably bright."

Layton gives him the middle finger and finishes his glass because he obviously doesn't have much more to say, and I look back at Jas. I want him to tell the story of Valerian now, because he doesn't really seem interested in his threat.

"Well, it was about four years ago in a really fancy bar in New York - the kind with cocktails that cost more than a monthly subscription to my gym." Layton laughs softly. "Tell her why we were there, Jas."

Jas snaps his fingers and grins cheekily. "Yeah, right! Valerian thought it would be a brilliant idea to make a bet."

I raise both eyebrows doubtfully. This can't end well. Valerian and a bet? Oh no. "Which one?"

"It wasn't a bet, it was a challenge," interjects the rightful protagonist of the story, but then gestures for the others to continue.

"Our lord and master here claimed he could drink every drink on the menu without collapsing."

"Sounds like a terrible challenge," I say with a laugh, squeezing Valerian's hand to comfort him a little as we laugh at him. "I was young and stupid," he grumbles in offense, but an amused grin flits across his face. Jasper laughs out loud as if he thinks those words are madness.

"All right, then. So Valerian has worked his way through the entire drinks menu. From martinis and tequila with burning cinnamon sticks to beer and vodka. At some point... he got emotional."

I blink a few times. Valerian squeezes my hand tighter. "Emotional?"

Layton nods somberly. "He started writing and composing love poems himself in Italian and reciting them to a complete stranger."

I turn my head in disbelief to Val, who just shrugs his shoulders innocently and licks his lips with a grin. "It gets better," Jasper says. "When she corked him, he just found himself a new woman to harass with his drivel. And then the next one. By the end of the evening, every woman in the bar had heard Valerian's soft, sweet Italian voice. That's how he met Izabella, a good friend of ours. At some point, he stood barefoot on the bar and gave a speech about his rhymes and how society no longer enjoys art and doesn't value every brushstroke enough."

By now I can't take any more and I'm holding my stomach with laughter, and I feel like my hand is about to break off, I'm squeezing Valerian's fingers so tightly. "Val, tell me they're taking the piss."

He just shakes his head and takes a deep sip from his glass. "I refuse to say a word about these accusations, I won't comment on them."

"Yes, you will, my friend, because the best part is still missing." Layton also takes a sip.

Jasper claps his hands with laughter, as if he's just remembered how the story ends. "When we finally got him out of the bar, he didn't want to go back to our apartment. He wanted to go to Paris. Immediately. He pressed a few hundred dollars into a cab driver's hand and shouted at him: 'Monsieur, take me to the land of baguettes and moustaches'!"

I almost topple off the sofa and Valerian supports me under his arms, pulls me protectively against his chest and buries his head in my neck. The warmth makes me feel good and I'm so busy laughing that I snuggle closer to him.

"And when the cab driver politely asked him not to shout at him and asked him if by Paris he meant some secret nightclub, Val swore at him and said, 'Quit being such a jerk' - as if the driver could get him across the water to Paris in no time."

Tears well up in my eyes and my stomach hurts. I dig my fingers into Valerian's leg, who looks at me as if he's never seen anyone laugh before. He looks happy too, but he remains silent. "What happened then?" I ask.

Jasper shrugs his shoulders. "At some point we put him in another cab and drove home. But only after he tried to persuade the doorman to sell him his jacket because he 'really needed the Parisian look'."

I don't think I can breathe anymore and finally feel like I'm choking as Valerian slowly shakes his head, raises his glass and mutters: "I hate you."

8

Silhouettes

Valerian

I dip the brush into the dark blue paint and draw the next stroke on my canvas. Despite the wired headphones connected to my Walkman, I hear someone enter the room behind me. I know it's her, but I pretend not to notice her.

I know her art class is always after mine. I know how she always almost sprints out of biology class to catch me in the art room. How she secretly watches me and thinks I won't notice. She spends her breaks outside with her friends to keep an eye on me, and yet I always do the same thing.

I smoke a cigarette and usually a second one too. But I also allow myself to look over at her from time to time. To watch and admire her. Her light brown, long, straight hair.

Sometimes she wears her glasses, sometimes not. Her brown, shiny eyes and her pink, soft lips.

And when our eyes cross, it's like fucking fireworks.

I always thought I was the observer. But in truth, we both are. I watch every move she makes, how she goes to the trash can or leaves the room to go to the bathroom. Most of the time she only does this because she is hoping that I will watch her and give her the tiny bit of attention she craves. She joins us and starts all sorts of conversations with Layton so she can be near me. She makes jokes with Jasper so I can laugh too.

At first I thought it was all about me. But I realized that she likes something about the three of us. Whatever it is, she can't let it go. Layton is her good friend, but Jasper is taken and I...

I'm just the observer.

Just like she is. Because even though she does all these things, she never dares to do more than that.

I turn my attention back to my canvas, but in the corner of my eye I see her putting her things down next to her seat, including a pile of books. At the top is her drawing pad.

She gives me a furtive glance, but I continue drawing.

We are alone in the room, but I assume she doesn't dare say anything because I still have my headphones in my ears and am wrongly concentrating on my work.

She leaves the room and I wait a few more seconds before I turn around and open the first page of her drawing pad.

I start to grin broadly.

I knew it.

It's a picture of me.

Bloody hell.

Of me, standing in front of my canvas, brush raised and headphones in my ear. The drawing isn't quite finished yet, but it's a picture she's seen of me again and again over the last few weeks and it must have inspired her so much that she wanted to draw it.

This girl...

My cock gets hard and presses against the fabric of my jeans.

Swallowing, I close the pad again, turn around and start to gather my things. Nervously, I turn the peak of my cap backwards and lick my lips. I pull out my headphones and block "The Way You Make Me Feel" by *Michael Jackson* out of my head. She's damn good at drawing, Marra is a creative talent.

She comes back into the room, this time with her friend Elara, and sits down in her seat. She pretends not to be interested in my presence, but I know better. A few weeks ago in computer science class, I sat next to Layton and Elara so we could do the assignments together. She pretended not to mind. Lay was talking to Elara, but it was the first conversation I had with Marra.

I remember when she pulled out her notebook and the drawing of our high school sports team caught my eye and burned into my eyes like a virus. Ever since I teased her about it, she knows I'm not a fan of our school team and her aloof behavior goes way against the grain.

"I like your artwork."

I look at her in surprise. Her brown eyes scrutinize me intently and I feel the corner of my right mouth twitch upwards slightly. She dares to speak to me?

The girl has plucked up her courage.

"Thanks, I've finished today," I say, and Elara looks back and forth between us with a grin before leaving the room with her paint tray, presumably to get some fresh paint.

"What was your task?" she asks.

"We were to draw our peace of mind and enhance it with colors." My drawing shows two people facing each other and are rather transparent, like silhouettes. They are surrounded by bright light that represents their souls. The background is dark blue, similar to the color of my eyes, at least that's what my art teacher says, and it's supposed to symbolize infinity and peace. The space between the silhouettes is marked by small colorful lines and spots, like thoughts floating from one to the other.

"Can you explain that to me?"

I knew this picture would be very intimate. I have never drawn anything so private and meaningful. Telling her about it felt strange and natural at the same time. As if I had painted it just for her, so that she would ask me about it. So that I could reveal my deepest thoughts to her. Maybe it's strange because we hardly know each other. We watch each other, we dream about each other, but that's all.

A silent dream.

But I trust her, for some indescribable reason.

I think she sees me. She has seen the Valerian King that I hide from most people, and she didn't even have to make an effort. She didn't have to speak a single word to me to know what I'm like.

That scares the hell out of me, but I'm not one to run.

"They are souls that somehow meet. And the colors - they show how they're connected," I begin, watching her closely as she looks at my painting with admiration, "Peace of mind isn't necessarily something you can only find within yourself, but also when you meet someone who understands you completely and respects your deepest depths instead of judging you."

I'm not interested in women. I rejected every girl who tried it with me without hesitation. The more girls found out about it, the fewer even tried. Maybe that's why Marra never went any further.

For me, she's the exception.

I don't believe in high school relationships like Jasper does.

I'm going to New York after graduation, and that's reason enough for me not to get involved in emotional relationships. But Marra...

"I didn't expect your portrayal to be so profound."

Her smile is warm and she looks at me as an artist and then at my work with genuine amazement.

Her words make me proud, but they also trigger an insecurity in me that I have never felt before. She recognizes everything I wanted to portray in this painting.

"Yeah? What do you like best?" She seems to have to think about my question for a bit, comes a little closer and looks at every inch of my canvas.

"Apart from the message, I like the unspoken love and connection between the two silhouettes. The colorful streaks of light that bring them together say more than words ever could." I smile softly at her words and my heart warms.

It's incomprehensible what this girl's presence does to me.

"But something is still missing." She reaches for the last brush I haven't put down yet and dips it into the bright yellow paint on the plate. My hand twitches, but then I pull back, trusting a woman I barely know and at the same time know to be a great talent and a gentle soul.

"May I?"

I nod curtly.

"Always."

She gives me a genuine smile, and the small dimple on the left side of her face appears. She is beautiful.

She places the fine brush over the two silhouettes and draws thin lines of color across the canvas. As she walks away, I see two small stars light up side by side. They light up the dark blue universe.

"Now it's finished."

She puts the brush back down and turns to me with a smile. "Thank you," I say and awkwardly put my hands in the front pockets of my trousers. Part of me wants to kiss her here and now and show her that I do care that she has immortalized herself in my painting. But I just can't do that. The risk is too great. We can't be more than what we are.

"Does music help you paint?" Her genuine interest flatters me.

I nod. "You should try it too. It's like an escape from this damn city." It's no secret how much I hate this dump. The demons that lurk here. The people who have made my life here a living hell.

I just want to get away.

"At home, I often put on a Tina Turner or Madonna cassette. But it's never occurred to me to use a Walkman for that." She tucks a few strands of her hair behind her ear and bites her lower lip gently. I pull the cable headphones out of my Walkman, look at all the signs and details I've scribbled on it, and then hand it to her. She looks down at it in surprise.

"You can keep mine. At least then I'll know that all the great drawings that will one day be famous were supported by the magical power of my Walkman." She laughs hard and loud, a pitch I've never heard her use before, and then hesitantly reaches for it. "I don't think you'll be seeing any drawings of me later." I frown in surprise and cross my arms in front of my chest. "Why not? You're a great artist." Giggling and mortified, she shakes her head slowly and runs her fingers over the little paintings on my Walkman. *Hers.*

"I'm afraid not everyone will see it that way. I prefer to keep my artwork to myself, it's in good hands." I stare. "There will always be people you're not good enough for, Marra. That's why your life shouldn't be about whether what you want to do is what other people expect you to do." She looks up at me with widened eyes, her lips curled into a soft smile and her fingers wrapped tightly around the Walkman. "Jasper said something similar to me the other day," she murmurs softly and I give her an encouraging wink. "He's a smart boy. You should listen to him."

I turn and reach for my backpack as she carefully packs my gift into her bag and then bravely straightens her shoulders. "Thank you, Valerian. For the Walkman. And for your words."

I shrug nonchalantly and walk towards the end of the room, heart beating fast. "Thank you too, for completing my work."

She gives me a curt nod. I leave the room.

This time without my Walkman and with a feeling in my chest that I had never felt before.

And this moment has opened my eyes again.

No matter how much I long for Marra and watch her, even though she's the only girl I'm interested in - it has to stay the way it is.

Maybe I told her about the importance of my picture because she is the second silhouette. Maybe she is the person.

And finding out if she is my peace of mind would be torture. Because she's an Asheville girl. And she's here to stay. I'd rather leave behind a girl who once gave me a hard-on than leave my peace of mind in my own hell and turn my back on her. I'm going to New York and nothing can stop me.

She can't mean anything to me, even though it might already be too late for that.

That's why it has to end here.

91

9

Pancakes with cherries

Marra

My whole body aches as I open my tired eyes and turn onto my back. I look up at the ceiling and take a few deep breaths. Last night was like a fever dream.

My head is throbbing from all the alcohol we've downed, as if it were water, and my throat is burning.

I've won the battle against Valerian, obviously, and as I tilt my head slightly I realize that the fire in the fireplace has gone out by now. I hear birds chirping from outside and bright sunlight shining into the hut. There is also something else. Soft music and a gentle humming. I sit up with a groan and pull down my shirt, which had ridden up slightly.

I feel like I'm in my romance novels, which I not only read passionately but also collect.

Layton is in the kitchen, working at the stove, swinging the pan back and forth in his hand. He doesn't notice me at first because he has his back to me and is quietly singing along to the song on the radio, which he must have switched on. It's "Kiss" by *Prince*. I bite my lower lip to stop the soft smile and giggles trying to fight their way to the surface. He's shirtless but wearing a pair of gray sweatpants that he must have pulled out of his pocket.

If I remember correctly, I still have some clothes here that I always leave behind for emergencies. For both warm and cold days. Sometimes my parents thought it would be a great idea to spontaneously drive out to the hut and so I started to build up a small stock of clothes.

"Good morning," he says and turns to me with a smile. I sit down on one of the wooden stools at the kitchen island and try not to show how much effort this movement is taking out of me. "Hey," I reply casually.

"Where are the others?"

"Here," I hear behind me and the front door swings open. Jasper holds up a bag of fresh food and sets it down in front of me. Layton claps his hands enthusiastically and immediately fishes out the things he needs. Among them are cherries and strawberries, maple syrup and powdered sugar. "Has our snoring princess woken up too?" Valerian closes the door behind him, blocking out the wall of light that had previously fallen into the entrance area. He cleans the soles of his shoes on the doormat and then smiles broadly when he sees me.

I must look like a scarecrow.

But none of them mind, because he and Jasper come up to me and press a kiss to the corner of my mouth. "I don't snore," I vow, and Val laughs raucously. "I really don't. I've woken up at least three times because of Jasper," I continue. Jas turns to me in mock shock and presses a hand over his heart. "Not true at all! I have a perfect nasal septum." I giggle. "The prize for snoring champion clearly goes to Layton," Jas protests and Layton taps his forehead insultingly. "I think you're crazy. Valerian is the culprit."

Now a chaotic discussion breaks out. Val dramatically raises his arms in the air and shakes his head so vigorously that I'm worried he's going to fly off at any second. "I don't snore."

"Man, you almost blew the roof off. Stand by your victory."

He puts his hands on his hips theatrically and gives us a disappointed look. "You conspired against me, didn't you? First that embarrassing story yesterday and then now. It's bordering on character assassination." I pull him to me by the hand, place him on the stool next to me and press a kiss to his cheek. "No, we're your biggest fans - oh, mighty victor and ruler." He rolls his eyes, but he can't suppress the amused grin and ends up laughing out loud.

Layton sets a plate of pancakes down in front of us, next to it a bowl of cherries and strawberries and the maple syrup with the powdered sugar. "We'll have breakfast later. We're going for a walk, make a few calls," says Jas, quickly grabbing a cherry and then scurrying to the front door. Val digs a laptop with a modem out of his travel bag and winks at me. "There's hardly any net in here, we'll try outside." Layton interrupts his work and looks after them. "But you have a satellite phone, Val."

"Yes, but Jas doesn't. I don't know, we're off for now." I wave weakly at him.

"See you later," I say and they leave us alone again.

I take a pancake and decorate it a little with the fruit and syrup. "I guess work won't leave you alone?" He shakes his head silently. "Valerian has a few other projects besides our company to achieve his goal. Besides, Jasper and I have to check that our representatives are doing everything right."

The guys have made a lot of money since they left Asheville, and I know a lot of people work for them. But it looks like they're still doing a lot of the work themselves.

"And what's Valerian's goal?"

He shrugs and sits down next to me. "Only he knows." I have a feeling that's not all, but I don't press him to tell me more.

Why should he? After this weekend, I probably won't see them again anyway. We start eating in silence, but it's not weird or awkward at all. Quite the opposite.

Even though I've been taking turns with one or more men all night, it feels completely normal to sit next to him and eat breakfast. I don't even know what time it is, but it doesn't bother me. It's like an escape from the normal routine that characterizes my life. And this is what I have chosen. This is my home and nowhere would I enjoy the peace and quiet more than here. But I'm also allowed to treat myself to a break from time to time.

There's nothing wrong with that, is there?

"Can I ask you something?" He hesitantly takes a bite of his first pancake and I nod. "Don't you ever feel the need to get away from here?" I know Valerian hates this place and that there was never any other option for him but to get out of here. But Lay? I was a part of his youth and he had a lot of fun, I know that. New York has opened up new opportunities for him, that's for sure, but why does he hate this city?

"I think I've always been comfortable with the silence. The people can be exhausting, but I've learned to live with it. Plus, I supply the town with flower wreaths and other decorations for the holidays - it's a good income."

I take a few bites and realize how spellbound he is listening to me. So I carry on talking. "I don't need the hustle and bustle and I'd rather live in a small, real circle than a big one where most people can't stand me. It would be very different in New York."

"I can understand that, but be careful who you trust. Sugar and salt look identical, Marra. We just showed up in front of you and you let us into your family home. You gave us your body without doubting us." I start to grin broadly. I know he's trying to make me feel insecure, to test me. But I'm smarter than that.

"I trust you guys."

"But why?"

"We've been friends since we were young teenagers, Layton."

He shakes his head stubbornly. "We haven't been in touch for years."

"That's not important to me. You always showed me back then that you were loyal to me and that I was important to you, even if it never turned into anything more." I hold my breath for a moment and wait to see how he reacts to my words. He tilts his head a little and looks at me scrutinizingly. "I've always liked you, little Mar. I would never do anything bad to you."

I exhale with relief. "You see. I got involved with the right people."

"Yes," he begins, "but you have to remember that Jasper and Valerian can be different. They want you at least as much as I do and they don't know you nearly as well as I do. They're enjoying what's going on right now, but even as their best friend, I don't know how this is going to turn out."

I know what he means. We've agreed to enjoy a weekend with no consequences and no future. But neither of us knows what will really happen afterwards. In the end, we have no choice but to go back to our lives. That's how it has to be. But maybe it won't be as easy as we thought.

"Jasper is actually here for Jadie's wedding. Valerian came along because Jas more or less forced him to. I'm here because I never let my best friends do stupid things without me. But then we saw you again because Jas also thought it was a good idea to stop by for a reunion. I mean, what are the odds of a reunion and a wedding falling on the same weekend?"

"Pretty slim."

"Right. But it does, and all three of us got what we dreamed about at night when we were teenagers. But what about you?"

I roll my eyes and sigh in disappointment.

"God, Layton, I'm no different. I would never have gotten involved in something like this otherwise."

As I roll up a pancake and bring it to my mouth, syrup runs out and drips onto my chin and the exposed skin between my shirt.

Cursing, I put it back down and wipe it away with my index finger before licking it off. Lay follows my movements with a hungry look. Butterflies fly through my stomach like a tornado and a blush rises to my cheeks.

"Don't look at me like that," I say in a whisper, averting my eyes. He laughs and grabs my chin to pull my face back towards him. Then he wipes off more syrup with his thumb, which I must have missed. "It suits you. You should walk around like that more often."

I giggle, licking my lips, and freeze when he pushes his thumb into my mouth and looks at me invitingly. I close my lips around his finger and immediately taste the remaining syrup. He pulls it out again with a pleasant plop.

"Take off your shirt, little Mar." His voice is rougher and deeper than before, showing me how aroused he is. One look at his crotch is the final proof - a large bulge is forming under the gray fabric. I do as I'm told and let the shirt slide off my shoulders so that it lands on the floor and I'm sitting naked in front of him. His hungry gaze glides up and down my body, burning my skin. "Sit on the island and spread your legs."

I hop off the stool and onto the kitchen island, the cold stone making my body shiver, but I put one foot on the stool at a time and spread my legs like he said. He has a perfect, unobstructed view of my center.

"Fuck, girl, you look so fucking sexy," he murmurs, pressing his lips to mine. His tongue makes its way to mine and they circle each other, one hand on the back of his head, the other supporting me. My abdomen tenses excitedly and my heart beats wildly and irrepressibly against my ribcage. A few months ago, my mother and I baked a cake in this kitchen. Now I'm here with a man and I'm getting fucked.

How times change.

I can feel his fingers approaching my labia and sliding between them. With his other hand, he plays with my hard, erect nipples and I sigh against his mouth.

I'm wet and it's not long before he enters me with two fingers at once and his lips make their way into the crook of my neck. I let my head fall back and moan deeply and lustfully as he rubs my pearl and thrusts his fingers rhythmically into me while he gently sucks on my nipples with his lips.

I don't know where he learned to pleasure a woman like this.

Damn, I'm glad he can do it.

"Fuck," I murmur, and he straightens up in front of me. "You ready?" I nod bravely and without another second's hesitation, he pulls off his sweatpants. I take hold of his bulging shaft and slide my fist up and down, squeezing a little harder from time to time, and I can see from the look on his face that he likes it. "You can lead," he says roughly and I nod excitedly. "Mmm."

He takes a step closer to me so that his tip touches my slit, and I guide him up and down. My body shakes and quivers under the pleasure building from the friction, and I let out a stifled gasp. "Do you like that?"

"It feels kind of sensitive," I begin, focusing on the movement, "but also kind of like the best foreplay ever." Even when Valerian rubbed his cock between my labia yesterday, I almost burst.

I can't take it anymore and push Layton's cock deeper into my entrance, then I pull my hand away and nod at him. He moves his hips so jerkily and firmly that I gasp a little and slide backward, but it's a pleasant ache.

My eyes roll back and I bite my bottom lip.

"Hold on," he growls harshly and pushes deeper into me, harder, filling me all the way from the inside. He wraps one hand around my lower back to keep me from slipping, and with the other he grabs my left shoulder.

Our breathing is rapid, and I curl my toes as he finds a satisfying rhythm and fucks me so barbarically well I wish I could do nothing else.

"How am I supposed to stop after tomorrow?"

His words make my heart stop beating for a moment.

I don't answer, because what can I say? I don't even know myself what will happen after this weekend. And I can't tell him anything I'm not completely convinced of myself. I've never lied to Lay and I don't even want to start.

Layton and I have been horny for each other since we were teenagers, but we've skillfully ignored it. Now that we're letting our lust run wild, it's like we've never done anything else. Jasper was taken at the time, so I would never have tried anything with him for that reason alone. But it looks like he needed me as much as I needed him.

And, shit, Valerian has a tattoo that will always remind him of our conversation. How he revealed a part of himself to me that no one else ever knew. I always knew why Valerian never got involved with anyone. No girl has been able to wrap him around her finger. Asheville is not his home.

I realized that early on, and yet every time I got to spend a little time with him, I wished it were different.

And this weekend gives me a preview of a life I could have had. Somehow.

Certainly not with all three of them. But maybe with one.

Either with Layton, a partner and friend at the same time, who gives me pure trust.

Or Valerian, the possessive one with the captivating look and the attitude of wanting to protect me from everything and everyone.

And Jasper would be a partner who only has eyes for me, is calm and understanding and wants to be the first to pull me into bed at home.

A life with all of them would be interesting - but it's hopeless.

"We still have time," I try to cheer us both up. Because this weekend is coming to an end.

A wave builds up inside me and I claw into his skin, looking for a way to save him. But in vain. Tears sting my eyes as he bites my neck and his body trembles. We come at the same time, he moans, I hold my breath to keep from screaming, and he quickly pulls out of me.

"Thank you for trusting me, Marra."

Then he presses a soft kiss to my temple and runs his hands over my body. I swallow hard, because his words trigger a warmth in me that speaks for nothing good.

I mustn't fall in love.

But then the warmth is gone again when I see his expression slowly change. He frowns and moves away from me a little, giving me a quick glance.

Awkwardly, I stay where I am, my chest still rising and falling rapidly, trying to figure out what's suddenly going on.

"Why didn't you open up to me back then, but you did to Jasper?" The look he gives me after his words eats a huge painful hole in my chest. My lips part and I want to say something, but I'm not even close to knowing what.

"I would have helped you experience new things. To be unpredictable. To get out." His voice is calm but I would never miss how much confusion and pain lies within it.

Fear settles on my limbs and I swallow hard because I don't want to hurt or upset him. Lay and I tried a few things as young teenagers. Smoking weed, my first sleepover with a boy even if it was with other friends, drinking alcohol... but then we drifted apart and what remained was Marra, sitting dutifully at home in her room with only a pale memory of these things.

"I was young and didn't know what I wanted. Jasper just saw what I never wanted to admit to myself. My inner rebellion to break the rules I set for myself." He props himself up on the island slab and eyes me bleakly. His eyebrows are drawn together thoughtfully and his arms are tense. "And now you know what you want?"

I shrug my shoulders. "I know I want this weekend."

"And after that?"

I don't answer directly, averting my gaze and looking for something in the room to latch onto. I shouldn't be ashamed of my will and my decision, because they are in line with the agreement. But it's still not easy to say it to his face.

"After this, I want my peace."

Our eyes meet and the amber of his eyes has lost all its sparkle as he looks at me long and hard. I hope he can see that I never want to hurt him. Even the fact that I didn't turn to him as a young girl was a problem of my own inner struggle and not because I didn't trust him.

"Go take a shower, we have to leave for the wedding soon." He pulls up his sweatpants and disappears out the front door, leaving me behind with a fat lump in my throat.

10

Steam bath

Jasper

Valerian hands me one of his Malboro cigarettes and I put it between my lips before holding up the lighter and lighting it.

I take a deep drag and close my eyes for a moment.

Shit, I'm not in the mood for this damn wedding. But having Marra with us makes me a little happier, and I think I might even have fun. Everything is fun with Marra - it always has been. I still remember the few moments when I made fun of her and joked with her. I'm pretty sure she stayed away from me at some point because she thought Jadie was jealous and didn't think Marra was funny.

Jadie really liked her. Although they didn't have much to do with each other, she never said a bad word about Mar and was always happy when she saw us laughing together.

I think that's awkward, but Jadie is... Jadie.

At first, Marra didn't even know I was taken. We met through our seatmates in geography class, and it wasn't until I started showing up regularly with hickeys that she realized she couldn't have me. I have to admit it was very funny when she saw me and Jadie together at one point, both with hickeys and very familiar, and she put one and one together. She should have seen the look on her face.

In the weeks that followed, she went to great lengths to show Jadie that she didn't want anything from me. I think she felt guilty because she always got on so well with me and didn't know that my girlfriend was watching us laugh and spending the lessons doing other things than listening.

Jadie herself even sought out Marra to get to know her better. At the time, I thought Jadie was looking for a candidate for a threesome. We had wild conversations about this from time to time, but as soon as I got the feeling that Jadie had it in for Marra, I turned it down. At the time, I didn't think she was cut out for that kind of thing - the delicate young girl in a threesome?

Never.

Maybe it's different now, but back then I wanted to keep her out of it.

But whenever she wasn't there, something was missing. Geography without Marra was boring. In the three years that we saw each other regularly, I realized how much I actually liked her. So much so that I broke up with Jadie just before we graduated because it just didn't feel right. Marra didn't really run in our circles, she didn't have any stoner or drinking friends, so she didn't notice the breakup. Then I found out she was moving to Weaverville, into a small apartment, and I decided to accompany my boys to New York. They tried for months to persuade me to come with them, but as long as I was with Jadie, it was out of the question for me. Tying myself down to another girl shortly after the breakup, to someone as beautiful as Marra, wouldn't have been good for me. I needed to find myself, spend a few years with my boys. New York was the perfect escape.

The wedding invitation and the letter inviting us to the reunion came just in time. Valerian and Layton think I just dragged them along for support. But each of us has a dark secret.

Mine is that I came mainly in the hope of seeing Marra again. I tried to convince myself that I left her behind for the right reasons. But she still has no husband, no family of her own. Besides, I know how addicted Lay and Val were to her in their youth. I had to take them with me.

And everything has turned out better than I imagined.

And at the same time, it's a huge disaster.

I think we've all lost a part of ourselves with her. I've been thinking all morning about how it can be that we all relate to her on such a deep level. I mean, it's incredible how well we work together. It's impossible for four people to be so passionate and friendly towards each other.

But I can't find any other solution to this other than we left a part of us in Asheville many years ago and that part was waiting for today. We all fell in love with her.

And we somehow never got away from it.

I don't want to say I still love her.

But just the sight of her makes my cock plump and stiff. Everything inside me aches when I can't touch her.

And I'm pretty sure it won't be as easy as we thought to leave this city behind. For the second time.

Maybe it was a mistake to come back after all.

"Izabella won't stop calling me," Valerian curses, looking at his satellite phone with a furrowed brow. I watch him for a moment as he switches it off completely and then puts it in his pocket.

"Do you really think it's a good idea to ignore her?" He just shrugs his shoulders, as if the subject leaves him completely cold. But I know how much it bothers him. The door opens and Layton steps out to us, his hair disheveled and his lips swollen. I start to laugh out loud.

"Looks like you two had a good time."

A wide smile forms on his lips and he leans against the wooden porch. "The syrup on her skin was to blame."

Valerian gives him a dirty look, but Layton ignores him.

"Judging by the look on your face, I'd say you're really fucked, bro," he grumbles to Val.

He grunts in a bad mood, his black shirt is tucked into his dark pants and he's wearing a cap over his blond hair.

"Don't act like you're not totally addicted to her too," I defend him, but Lay shakes his head. "I never stopped being addicted to her. I've just gotten used to hiding it since I was fourteen."

Yeah, that son of a bitch had it even harder than we did. He was always near her. Always close and yet always far away.

"How about we just kidnap her and drag her along?" suggests Valerian, and there's silence for a few seconds.

Actually, that's not such a bad idea, but I don't believe in illegal kidnapping and coercion. And I think that what happens here should stay here. Marra got involved because it's only for a weekend. I promised her there would be no future and no consequences. She doesn't even really know who she's dealing with here.

And I always keep my promises.

"We can't do that. She belongs here."

I can feel Valerian's killing stare. He's always been a jealous, stubborn and possessive person. With others, he's good at hiding it and wears a mask of indifference, looking bored or disinterested practically all the time, but not with us. Valerian is creative, passionate and puts his whole heart into things he really wants.

"You can't have her, Val. She belongs to peace." And he knows better than anyone that he is not Peace. I stomp out my glowing cigarette butt.

"Speaking of which, didn't you want to talk to Klaus on the phone?" asks Layton, cleverly diverting the subject. Val had a few calls to make or emails to answer on our walk, and one of those urgent people was Klaus, it's true. But since I already know what he wants to tell him, I end the conversation at this point and go into the house to find our little girl.

When I hear the hissing behind the bathroom door, I briefly consider what to do, but then I open the door and step into a wall of pure sauna heat and steam.

My goodness, how hot is her shower?

The bathroom has wooden walls, small ceiling lamps and brown tiles. She doesn't notice me and I take advantage of the surprise effect, take off my clothes and watch her. She has a perfect body. She moves delicately and gently, but she also has a certain rough hardness about her. Her thighs and hips are round and firm, her bottom is plump. She has soft curves, a not particularly large bust and slender calves. Her brown hair is darker at the roots than at the ends, where it tends to be light blonde.

I know a lot about her and I'm sure she'd be very surprised.

She learned to ride as a little girl because her mother had a black horse - so I particularly enjoyed it when she rode me for hours tonight, moving her hips like a pro.

Two years in a row, she fell off her horse and broke her left wrist and the next year her right wrist. A short time later, she broke her ankle. Do I feel like a stalker? Maybe a little.

Now she sees me, but she doesn't flinch in horror, but opens the shower door for me with a flattering smile. I'm pretty sure she's driving me crazy, but she'd better not know that. She presses herself firmly against the shower wall and I stand under the jet of water. She must have a CD player, because "Do you wanna touch me" by *Joan Jett & the Blackhearts* is blaring loudly through the room.

"Hey," she says quietly and purses her lips with a grin as I lift her hand to my lips and place a gentle kiss on it. "Baby," I reply, noticing how she flinches a little at this term of endearment.

"I'm glad you're keeping me company for a while."

"Anytime you want, baby," I say with a laugh and reach for the soap, put a little on my palm and then grab her arm. Roughly, I pull her towards me and lather her hair.

We say nothing as my cock gets stiffer and stiffer and presses against her stomach. She looks up at me, watching me through those light brown eyes and thick lashes, like she doesn't know what I'm going to do next.

Spoiler alert: I'm going to fuck her.

Hard and animalistic against the tiled wall of the shower.

After a little time has passed and I've allowed her to soap my hair too, she stands on her tiptoes and brings her lips close to my ear. The way she touches my body makes me hold my breath for a moment. My cock twitches and I want to sink myself deep inside her.

"Are you angry with me?" she asks shyly. Perplexed, I lean back and slowly shake my head. Then I understand.

Grinning mischievously, I ask: "Because you let Layton fuck you without us?" She nods dumbly.

"God, no, baby."

"Promise?"

I reach for her delicate hands and give them a quick squeeze before nodding decisively.

"How about this for proof?" I turn her around, place her palms flat against the wall and push her upper body forward a little. Then I push her legs further apart with one foot and run my hands over her damn sexy ass.

"They won't be mad if I take you here and now, either." She gasps, but through the rippling water and the music I almost don't notice.

"I told you a while ago that you can't please anyone, baby. Not even us, no matter how nicely we respond. We always want more from you because you're so amazing." She bites her lower lip, nodding weakly, and turns her head crookedly in my direction. She's so perfect - the kind of woman you want for your entire life.

I reach for my cock and look at the piercing I got a few years ago. Val and I were pumped to the brim with alcohol when Layton dragged us to a tattoo parlor in revenge for another prank. My drunken self thought it would be a good idea to get my dick pierced.

Much to Lay's displeasure, however, I haven't regretted it for a single day. The girls like it. Well, most of them.

I think it touches a spot in them or intensifies the passionate feeling - or some shit. Anyway, I know Marra likes it too.

I thrust into her with a sweeping jerk and she slips off with one hand. She quickly catches herself again, bends down even further and bends her knee a little. I grab her by the hips to stabilize her and thrust into her again. Now I hear her moaning loud and hard, which makes me grin. "Fuck, yes," she curses and I thrust into her again. Her pussy tightens, closing around my cock with relish and I moan. The friction this creates almost catapults me into another realm.

I get faster and faster, but I don't overdo it. I enjoy how warm her pussy is and how willingly she takes me inside her.

"Do you still think I might be mad at you?"

She shakes her head absently and I could swear her mind has long since disappeared into the clouds.

"Marra?"

She groans loudly.

"No, I don't think so. Go on, please."

That's exactly how I like her.

I lose myself in her, fuck her until I get bored of the position. I turn her towards me, lift her onto my hips and sink my cock back inside her. Pressed against the wall, I thrust in and out of her. Her back rubs against the tiles and I notice her face contort in pain, but since she doesn't tell me to stop, I keep fucking her.

Her fingers bury themselves in my hair and she pulls on it, probably to relieve the pressure on something else.

"I'm about to come, Jas," she breathes.

Her words alone make my cock twitch painfully and it swells inside her more and more.

Fucking Jadie was sweet - something you do as a couple. Yes, she was kinky and wanted to talk me into a threesome or role play every now and then but it doesn't come close to sex with Marra.

Because with Marra, I know that every fiber of my body is happy. With Jadie, I longed for her. Now I have her and I want nothing more than that.

With Mar, I'm the Jasper I've always wanted to be.

"God, you're so fucking perfect." A load of cum signs up to spurt inside her, but before it gets that far, I pull out of her, matching her trembling cry, and her quivering legs give out from under her as I set her down. I prop her up against the wall and as my cum flows down the drain along with the water, I kneel down to her. "You did a great job, baby."

As she sits there, I can see the red welts on her back.

"I'm sorry about that. Come with me, I'll take care of you."

11

Best wedding ever

Marra

I'm glad of the decision Jasper has made. He fished a long satin slip dress in a smoky shade of lavender out of my dresser and gently slipped it over me, as if he was afraid I might burst at any moment.

He didn't even tighten the strings on my bare back after rubbing me with ointment and kissing the streaks from the shower wall that were left on my back. Putting on my shoes was similar. He kept kissing my legs from the feet up and gently closed the strap. I'm not really used to this from him, but I more than enjoyed this side of him. I might have deliberately contorted my face from time to time, as if he was hurting me, to make him even more tender and loving.

But then I was allowed to put my hair up myself, after which he clipped two little butterfly hair clips into my hairstyle, but, wouldn't you know it, I also had to carry my bag myself.

What a Stone Age man, he could at least have taken it off me.

Luckily for me, the three men are back in their dark suits and look damn good in them. In the past, I would never have dreamed how serious and classy they could look.

Because they are damn good in them.

Harmonious music lulls the ceremony into a romantic mood and Valerian intertwines our fingers while Layton sways rhythmically back and forth. Jasper has disappeared somewhere among the guests, I assume to talk to Jadie's family, but the other two have dutifully stayed with me.

There are other people here from our school days, and that makes me a little nervous. After all, I'm here with three men. And then with the three men who went to New York a few years ago to start a new life. One of them happens to be the bride's ex-boyfriend and another is her absolute enemy. Because Jadie and Valerian could never really stand each other.

Layton and Jadie probably don't even really know each other, and that will probably confuse the guests even more. And then there's me. That's probably the strangest thing.

Sighing, I glance through the rows and at the guests. Jadie and her groom are celebrating at a somewhat secluded spot in Asheville. A small castle, the Biltmore Estate, perfectly decorated for the wedding. An altar is set up in front of us and everything is decorated with white and yellow roses.

It reminded me a little of the color scheme from "Beauty and the Beast". The flimsy iron chairs we've been sitting on for an hour are damn uncomfortable, but they're better than standing and giving fake smiles to all these people, half of whom I don't even know.

"What are you analyzing?" Layton asks me, and I frown thoughtfully. My gaze wanders from one bouquet of flowers to the next and back and forth between the table arrangements. It happens automatically, as if I'm sizing up my competition.

Lay seems to notice and grins mischievously at me.

"You could have done better." I smile gratefully at him and lean back a little in my chair to find a comfortable position.

I sat next to him on the way here and he quietly held my hand, which was probably to show me that he no longer resents the conversation we had earlier.

Which makes me feel very relieved.

"I hate weddings," Val grumbles, squeezing my hand tightly.

"Have you ever been to one?" I ask with interest, and my two neighbors exchange a quick glance, then he shakes his head.

"But he will be soon," Lay adds quietly. Smiling gently, I ask: "Who's getting married?"

Valerian doesn't think it necessary to answer and gives Layton a dark look. "A friend of ours from New York, but Val doesn't like the bride very much." I see, I understand. Strange.

"I've never been to a wedding," I say. I guess I just don't have enough friends for that, or I haven't kept in touch with the ones I have had well enough for anyone to invite me to their wedding. I'm absolutely terrible at keeping in touch, but I don't judge myself for it either. It's not really part of my world and I don't see it as necessary.

"I thought you regularly do the decorations and arrangements for events like this. Isn't the designer invited?" I frown at Valerian's question. "No. It doesn't work like that."

"Too bad," he replies with a shrug.

Suddenly I notice Jasper in the crowd, shaking hands with a man who must be Jadie's little brother. He has the same gray eyes, light brown hair and a wicked smile. They talk for a few minutes before Jasper moves on and greets a woman.

No one pays any attention to us, and I'm very glad of that.

Every now and then Layton gets a wave or a smile from old schoolmates, but he doesn't seem particularly keen to talk to them, as he just returns the smile and otherwise stays seated next to me.

"Can we go now?" I too am bored by now and wonder how anyone can waste so much time at such an important ceremony. If I was the bride and really loved my groom, I would want to marry him as soon as possible. And I wouldn't throw such a huge party.

Valerian strokes the back of my hand with his thumb and I give him a genuine smile as I look into his blue eyes. He has a mole on his left cheek, right between his nose and eye. When he puts his other hand on my thigh and strokes me gently, the heat awakens in me. I had my fun with Layton and Jasper this morning, but Valerian hasn't gotten very close to me since last night. Immediately, it starts pulsing between my thighs and I squeeze them painfully to ignore the sensation. I'd much rather be in the cabin right now, spending my time with them, neat and naked, than sitting here waiting for something I'm not really interested in.

Layton notices my physical reaction to Valerian's touch and gives me a crooked grin before leaning forward and resting his elbows on his knees to block my view.

Oh no.

They're not going to do that.

Or are they? Before I can think another thought, Val's hand slides under the fabric of my dress and finds its way to my throbbing center.

"Valerian," I whisper warningly and slide back and forth a little on the chair. "Just relax, yellow star. I'll take care of the rest."

Sighing and absolutely aroused by the meaningful nickname, I slide a little lower and let my dress slide up inconspicuously. No one is watching us anyway, and as long as I don't make a sound, it won't happen.

He brushes my fresh thong aside a little to give himself better access and I let out a hissing breath. These men are my downfall. "Spread your legs and keep your game face on." His mischievous grin will haunt my dreams long after this day is over - that's as sure as the Amen in church.

I open my legs as wide as the cut of my dress will allow and am suddenly infinitely grateful that it only reaches the middle of my thighs anyway. "I'm already wet."

His eyes twitch greedily and he licks his lips. "Shit, why the fuck did we come here?"

He runs two fingers over my wet pussy and plays with my pearl, causing me to whimper. I look around scrutinizingly, but no one has heard. Layton gives us an amused look and holds out his hand to me. I grab it and squeeze it so I can take it out on him instead of screaming it all out.

Val plays with my clit like it's his favorite toy, looking deep into my eyes and not breaking eye contact for a second. Shit, I'm so aroused. The fact that someone could catch us at any time doesn't make it any better and the forbidden makes my adrenaline pump.

"I love that you're always so wet for us, yellow star."

I'm shocked by his words for a second, but then I see the fire that flares in his eyes and I'm glad he's being honest with me. Men have never aroused me and touched my soul like they do. And I don't see how it could ever be any other way.

"Shit," Layton curses, turning his gaze to the crowd to avoid being distracted by us.

At this moment, Valerian inserts a finger into me and continues to play with my pearl with his thumb. My whole body is electrified and I feel warm as he adds another finger. Again and again he slides out to stroke my pussy, then continues the rhythm of expanding and sliding. I squeeze Layton's hand tighter and bite my lower lip with my teeth. Breathing heavily, I close my eyes. My nipples erect, and I'm glad you can't see it through the fabric. "That feels so good."

My voice sounds like I'm hoarse or completely out of it.

"How do you want me to fuck you later?" I'm unable to answer at first because I'm so perplexed and speechless from the violence of my feelings that I'm just enjoying his touch. But then he interrupts them briefly and I remember his question.

"On the porch." He continues the motion, circling my pearl with his thumb. My legs tremble slightly. "Go on?"

"I want to sit on your cock, and I want you to fuck me until it hurts." He bites my shoulder and guides his fingers out and back in faster. "I love it when you talk like that."

The pressure on Layton's hand intensifies.

"I'm looking forward to it," I sigh in anticipation of the next few hours.

He laughs and moves close to my ear. My breathing is choppy by now and I'm on the verge of cumming. Conversations like this are the beginning of every orgasm.

"You'll have to wait a little longer, yellow star, like a good girl."

"I'm always a good girl," I reply and even Layton laughs at my words. The friction against my pearl and the movements become harder, faster and more captivating. "Our good girl," murmurs Valerian.

And I let myself fall completely.

I come on Valerian's fingers, the orgasm shaking through my whole body.

Out of the corner of my eye, I notice how the scene around us slowly changes and the groups disperse. Jas suddenly stands next to Valerian and looks down at us, sees what we're doing and frowns. Then he seems to realize it and curses. Val pulls his fingers out of me and holds them in front of our eyes. They're shiny and wet. Lay pushes my dress back down so that everything is covered again and kisses my hand. But all my concentration is on Valerian, who takes his fingers with my slightly milky ejaculate into his mouth and licks them clean.

The music changes in the background and the murmuring of all the guests, who have now taken their seats, begins. I notice the bulge in Valerian's trousers and decide to reward him later for this highlight. "You guys are completely crazy," Jasper says to us before leaning back on the iron chair and looking ahead.

Valerian presses a fleeting kiss to my lips and puts an arm protectively around my shoulders. Still slightly dazed, I see the groom standing at the altar. The doors of the castle open and Jadie steps out into the majestic castle garden in a gorgeous white dress.

"The best wedding of my life," I hear Valerian murmur before I switch off my brain for a few minutes and watch the ceremony intently.

12

Castle wall

Valerian

I hate being in the center of attention and not on the sidelines where I can watch everyone. I don't like dancing anyway. But Marra held out her hand and gave me a wait-and-see look after Jadie and her loser groom said yes. I practically had no other chance.

I could never resist the pleading in her loving eyes or turn down something that would make her happy. Layton may have laughed at me because he knows how much I loathe it, but I don't care. Fuck him.

I'm here, with Marra, rocking her to the beat of the music. I don't know how I do it, but I have a feeling it doesn't look as bad as I feared. I never said I couldn't dance - I just don't like it.

Old memories of my mother come flooding back and I shudder. She taught me to dance when I was little and twirled around the house with me for hours until my stepfather came home and the atmosphere became almost unbearable.

If he hadn't died a long time ago, I probably would have killed him one day.

I look back at Marra, who is laughing happily, our hands are clasped tightly and our bodies are snuggled together. We make a good dancing couple. But if she knew who she was spending her time with, she'd probably run away. A lot has changed since we moved to New York. I'm not the man I used to be, and part of me is scared because I can fool her into thinking I'm the same man I used to be. New opportunities have opened up for me. New worlds that I didn't know before. I've found my way and I'm glad that I have two loyal friends by my side. Klaus Diabolus is not to be trifled with when it comes to loyalty and discretion.

Marra must not be dragged into this whole story under any circumstances. She mustn't know anything about any of this.

This is not a world for her, even if I would love to kidnap her and drag her away with me.

I don't feel as comfortable with any woman as I do with her.

She understands me, she always has, and touches a sore, deeply buried spot in me that I thought had been extinguished.

But it was always there, just hidden, until it saw Marra again. The second silhouette in my picture. My peace of mind. A realization that I never wanted to accept or acknowledge. Because that would only lead us all to ruin.

"Get ready," I whisper to her, and she tears her eyes open, pumped full of adrenaline, before I fling her from my arm and then turn her until I lean down to her and look deep into her eyes. There's a genuine laugh on her adorable lips and I feel sick.

I want to fuck her so *fucking* badly. Her pussy was wet and pulsing as she willingly spread her legs for me. And like the good little girl she is, it only made her hornier that people can catch us doing it.

Did I say good girl? I mean corrupted.

But she doesn't like to let on.

Her laugh is the most beautiful thing I've ever heard in my life. And her smile... it feels like a dream. She passes on her happy feelings and moments to me.

What a lucky guy I am.

My cock twitches and presses excitedly against my suit trousers. I suddenly become aware of these incredibly itchy and uncomfortable pants again and tense my neck uncomfortably.

I'll probably have to get used to them slowly, because I'll have to wear them quite a lot in my future job.

I sigh.

Marra looks at me questioningly as she snuggles up to me and we still move like smooth water to the music. Everything feels so easy with her. "What's wrong, Val?"

I can't tell her the truth, so I spin a lie. Or rather, a question I've been wanting to ask her for a while.

"I know you fancy all of us. Layton, as your dear childhood friend, Jasper as your forbidden treasure and me, as your unstoppable observer. But I'd like to know how it feels for you to have all of us now. All three of us in one go. Is it hotter? More exciting?" Her cheeks immediately turn red and she lowers her eyes in shame.

Laughing, I lift her chin, give her a quick kiss and then lead her into a spin before pulling her back towards me. Now she's standing with her back against my chest, which I take advantage of to get close to her ear. "You know you don't have to be pretty in front of me. What else do you want from us?"

She bites the inside of her cheek naughtily and raises her head so that she looks deep into my eyes. By now at the latest, she should realize how hard my cock is and how little I can wait to sink into her again. She rubs her bottom against my crotch and I growl deeply. My body feels like it's filled with electricity. Ready to be shocked at any moment.

"I'll take anything I can get, Val. But I've always wanted to...swallow." Oh, shit.

"Yeah?"

I twirl her around again so we're dancing chest to chest again. "Yeah."

I gently bite her earlobe. I bet she's already wet again. I resolve to give her that taste today. She deserves everything she wants. But there's a question working its way up my throat like a mountain hiker.

"What are you going to do after this weekend?" I ask, and immediately a panic sets in that I'm not used to. Will she just forget about us again? She says nothing for a few seconds and we enjoy the soft music before she takes a deep breath. But she says nothing, remains silent.

Well, actually, I have no right to ask her that or worry about it. I'm the one she's least likely to have a future with. Unfortunately, I'm just as aware of that as everyone else on this planet. And that pisses me off.

Jasper is a dirty old bitch. I know exactly why he made that suggestion to Marra. Whether it was out of selfishness or team spirit. He was hoping to see her again. But the promise he made her... I'd like to rip his head off for that. A weekend without consequences is the right thing to do. *I know that.*

This is about freedom. About taking what we've all always wanted. Even if the four of us go back to New York, how is that going to work? She can't have a relationship with all of us. The reality is different.

"Don't forget the rules we set," she demands, and I want to push her away. Anger builds up inside me and for a moment I see black. We're just an exception for her, a pact. A worthless fuck.

I know that's what we agreed. These are the rules.

It's the right way.

It has to be this way, Valerian.

I want to smash everything and everyone that crosses my path.

I pull her off the dance floor, regardless of whether anyone sees us. One of the guys will definitely be keeping an eye on us, but I don't care.

"What are you doing? Where are we going?"

I don't answer and continue to drag her through the castle garden until we've disappeared around a corner. We're standing on the terrace, a delicate railing borders the area, but that's enough for me. No one can see us from here, the wedding guests are shielded by the castle's protruding façade. She almost falls over on her heels, but I pull her on. Just a little bit.

My heart is racing and the rage that tears me apart and hurts me so much is raging inside me. I have to get rid of it. Now and immediately.

Her look is confused, but she doesn't seem afraid. That's good.

She must notice my change of mood, but she says nothing about it and doesn't stop me as I pull up her dress and expose her beautiful legs. As I press my fingers on her thong, I realize to my satisfaction that she really is almost dripping with arousal and I pull at the fabric until it tears. She gasps in shock and presses her legs together. "What's wrong with you all of a sudden?"

Ignoring her words, I unzip my trousers and reach for my swollen cock. A drop of pleasure glistens on my tip and I stroke my shaft up and down a few times.

"What's wrong? Don't you want to enjoy the weekend? It's almost over, yellow star." She looks around, frowns and bites her lip. She really should stop this habit.

"Did I hurt you?" she asks and I laugh out loud.

I shake my head in amusement. "Not at all, no. You were just telling the truth."

"Valerian, I know we..." she begins, but I put my hand over her mouth to stop her from continuing. I don't want to hear what she has to say, not a single word. Not about how much she likes me and how well we harmonize with each other, but that it simply can't be and shouldn't be.

Because I know that myself, but I've been living in an illusion for the last few hours and avoiding the truth.

This is one of our last moments together.

So let's enjoy it, shall we?

I penetrate her hard and brutally so that she is pressed against the rough stone façade. She gasps loudly and claws into my shoulders. My hand is still on her mouth and her nostrils flare as she tries to regulate her breathing.

"I'm just going to take what I want, just like you."

Again, I thrust deep inside her. I come almost to the hilt and immediately penetrate her again. She whimpers under my hand, but it doesn't even occur to me to take her away.

I was just talking about how much I love her laughter and her voice. That was a lie, because I hate it.

Because she will forever remind me of what I can't have.

A woman who really wants me. The woman I want more than anything.

I work my way into her again and again, fucking her hard and painfully against the castle wall. She'll never be able to forget this moment again. Who gets fucked against a castle at a wedding? I like to say that this doesn't happen often.

"Do you like that, little star?" I watch as she lowers herself against me, her eyes rolling back and her wetness spreading over my cock. I know she likes it. She's into this fucked up shit.

She's perfect.

I twitch inside her, my breathing heavy by now, but I keep fucking her. Then I pull out of her, run my tip through her pussy and her legs shake. She grabs my ass and squeezes it against her, and I slide back into her, making me so horny that I'm about to cum. "My girl."

My anger slowly ebbs away and I start to enjoy the moment to the full. I've given in to the blackness for too long and relinquished control without holding back. This is not good.

When I finally remove my hand from her mouth, she lets out a gasping breath, moans loudly and digs her fingers firmly into my ass. "Whatever's wrong with you, you're fucking hot."

"Thanks, baby."

13

Escaping the ex-girlfriend

Jasper

I've been standing on the steps to the castle terrace for at least twenty minutes to give them a little time to themselves. I saw the blackness in Valerian's eyes when they rushed off.

I told Layton I'd take care of it, because he would have just stormed in and taken away Valerian's chance to calm down. But I'm standing guard and I know Val would never hurt her. He just needs to remember who he is again. He's in a crisis, and it's not the first time he's acted rashly.

Lay doesn't understand this as much as I do. But I trust Valerian and I know what he needs to do to calm down. Marra is a strong girl, she'll be able to handle it. She probably even likes the cold version of our friend. After all, she got involved in our deal for a reason.

Suddenly Jadie appears next to me, her grandmother Bridget hanging on her arm and the two of them are chatting happily. Not wanting to shout rudely at the bride on her wedding day and block her path, I quickly walk ahead until Mar and Val come into my field of vision. She's on her knees licking the cum off his cock and he's got his head tucked back with relish. Grinning, I saunter towards them and when Marra notices me, she stands up quickly.

Her dress has slipped, the strings holding her dress together at the back are loose.

"If I were you, I'd get dressed inconspicuously again. The bride and her grandmother will be here any minute."

Well, maybe I didn't stop Jadie because I want to provoke a clash.

That would be too funny.

Valerian carefully repacks his cock. I walk towards Marra and retie her dress, but I can already hear Jadie's unpleasant voice.

Fun.

"The wedding planner really has thought of everything. And the location is really fantastic, don't you think, Grams?"

They walk around the corner together, first looking into the distance at the lush green of the lawn, then their eyes fall on us. Marra's dress is still relatively loose and Valerian is still busy zipping up his trousers, which doesn't leave Jadie much room for interpretation.

All her features slip away and she watches us with her jaw dropped as we clean up the mess. "Oh dear," I hear her grandmother purr softly and I laugh. "Sorry about that. But we just couldn't hold back in such a romantic atmosphere," says Valerian, putting an arm around Marra's shoulders. Jadie looks back and forth between us, confused.

Then horror is reflected in her face.

"Don't get upset, doll. Today is your special day." I know how much my words have upset her.

And I've made up my mind now.

I think it's *disgusting* to invite your ex-boyfriend to your wedding.

So I'm going to let her know.

"So this," she begins, pressing her lips tightly together. I notice how Marra's cheeks turn red and how Jadie looks back and forth between us. Like she wants to chase us through the castle.

"How dare you! Have you no decency?" I grab Marra by the wrist and go to pull her past Jadie, with Valerian in tow, but Jadie lunges and slaps my cheek hard with the palm of her hand.

Ouch.

"Get out of here," she yells at me and a wide grin appears on my lips. This only seems to annoy her even more, because she angrily lifts up the hem of her dress and grabs her expensive shoe. "I invite you to my wedding and you do this embarrassing and outrageous shit to me? Bringing people like that to my special day? And then her of all people? Fuck you, Jasper Bailey." I drag Marra behind me as I chase after Valerian, laughing at the top of my lungs. Apparently, after all these years, she actually does have a problem with Marra.

She throws her shoe at us and chases after us, limping, but it doesn't even come close to hitting us. Mar and Val are laughing too and I can see tears forming in her pretty eyes.

When we arrive at the rows of seats, the dance floor and the band, the guests look at us, startled and confused. "Jasper, watch out!" At Marra's warning, I duck before the second shoe whizzes over me and grazes my hair.

Layton jumps up from his seat, startled, the car keys already in his hand, and pushes a few people aside to make room for us to escape. Adrenaline pumps through my body and I suddenly feel so light and... happy.

Yes, teasing my ex and fleeing her wedding while she throws her shoes, then flower wreaths and chairs at us fills me with euphoria and freedom.

She really should see a therapist for aggression.

I'll send her my contacts as soon as I get back to New York.

"Have another fulfilling marriage," I shout loudly, raising my thumb over my shoulder before I get into the car behind Marra, laughing, and Layton crunches into the gas.

"Woohoo." Valerian shrieks through the car, all the old man and his darkness seemingly forgotten. Our little girl presses her palms to her glowing cheeks, a cheeky grin on her face and a glint of joy in her eyes. "That was amazing."

I nod and intertwine our fingers before looking through the window to see the castle getting smaller and smaller. "You guys really are crazy. Marra, you know this is going to spread like wildfire in Asheville." Layton glances back at us through the rearview mirror, but she just shrugs indifferently.

"At least they'll have something to talk about."

I look at her for a moment, seeing the beautiful girl who has us all wrapped around her finger. She would change all our lives, save them and destroy herself in the process.

I avert my gaze. I was right to leave her here as a teenager. To let her believe that I never had real feelings for her. And maybe, just maybe, I was afraid of how far we would go if I confessed my feelings to her first. The whole time I was taken, we got to know each other better, had fun together and enjoyed classes together, but more was never an option. How was I supposed to know how she would react to me if I stood in front of her as a single man? Let alone how *I* would have reacted.

"We could do this more often," Val warbles and makes himself comfortable in his seat.

Yes, he's right.

But it will never happen again and we all know that.

14
Skinny Dipping

Marra

The wind is blowing through the whole car and loose strands of hair keep whipping into my face. I've leaned my feet out of the open window and am lying half-stretched out on the back seat, my head on Jasper's lap.

We've been driving for about forty minutes with loud music and good humor. Val seems to be doing better because he sings along loudly to every song, keeps looking back at us and I notice the sparkle in his blue eyes when he looks at me.

I don't blame him for the brief lapse.

The question "What then?" drives me crazy too and I can understand that my words have upset him so much. The subsequent scene with Jadie was incredibly uncomfortable for me, but at the same time I also felt free and untouchable. For the first time, I didn't care what others thought about me. I had fun doing what I did and I was able to enjoy it to the fullest.

It feels like a rush.

Is that really me?

It's strange that I find it so easy to get out of myself and escape my habits, but actually it was much needed. I like my life, but when I lie in my bed at night, stroking Leo and lost in thought, I imagine what it would be like if I had made different choices in life. What I would be like as a person if I didn't always put myself last, but that's not so easy when you've been doing it since you were a child.

The pursuit of peace and reason has been ingrained in me from an early age. I was never a loud or demanding child, and my parents always made me feel that my reason and shy soul were a virtue.

But I long to break out. Just for this weekend.

After Val finds the compartment with all my cassettes, and really inspects each one as closely as if he were trying to solve a murder case, he decides on one that I haven't played in a long time.

"I Love Rock'N'Roll" by *Joan Jett & the Blackhearts* echoes through the car and Jas taps his fingers to the rhythm on my shoulders. His gaze is dreamily directed outwards, but he nods his head to the beat.

Before I can speak to him, Valerian's excited voice echoes through the car. "What's your cat's name, yellow star?"

I blush instantly and bite my lower lip. "He doesn't have a special name." Val turns to me and gives me a scrutinizing look. "Speak up."

Layton also seems interested and keeps looking at me through the rear-view mirror. "I named him after someone I used to know." Jasper opens his eyes and laughs. "And who was that someone?"

"It was just a little boy from my childhood, okay?"

"What's the bloody cat's name, Marra?"

"Leo." Valerian snorts and looks ahead at the road again. "Sounds like an idiot." I laugh and shake my head. "You seriously named your cat Leo?" I shrug innocently and Layton averts his eyes too, as if disappointed by this fact.

When I look back at Jasper, I see that his face is dreamily turned towards the window again and he's watching the trees rushing past us.

I let him be, assuming he probably needs a few minutes to get all his thoughts in order.

After the song is over and Valerian begins his second search, eventually ending up with *Bon Jovi* singing "You Give Love A Bad Name", I gently stroke Jas's arm.

"Are you okay?" I ask him and he nods silently. Concerned, I turn my head a little on his lap and stretch it in his direction so I can look at him better. "Are you sure?"

This time he looks at me, his warm brown eyes fixed on my face.

His cold and unthinking gaze makes me nervous, and his finger stops tapping my skin to the rhythm of the music. "It's just this stupid wedding."

I understand that he's upset about being at his ex-partner's wedding. I mean, no one likes to experience something like that, right?

But then why did he come at all?

"Do you want to talk about it?" I ask gently. Because even though this weekend is about having fun, I want to be there for them. They've spoiled me in every possible way for several hours and I can at least give them something back. Caring.

"There's not much to say, baby. After we broke up, I ran off to New York and didn't think about her once. I was fine without her." I feel like he wants to say more, but he doesn't and continues to look at me in silence before turning away with a slight smile. "Why did you break up?"

He's silent for a few seconds, and all I can hear is Valerian singing along to the song, patting Layton on the shoulder repeatedly to get him in the right mood.

"Because of you."

I take a surprised, shaky breath and turn away now too, looking down at my feet sticking out the car window. I've always tried to make Jadie feel like I don't want anything from Jasper. Which was a lie, remembering my fast beating heart from back then, but I held back. He was with a girl I got on relatively well with. We didn't do much together, but we didn't have a problem with each other either.

The last thing I wanted was for them to break up, and then because of me.

"I had feelings for you and Jadie realized that. I thought it was unfair to her and I felt like a coward. That's why I let her go." I swallow.

"Why didn't you tell me?"

I'm pretty sure the boys can't hear our conversation. They're so engrossed in their karaoke and the ride that they probably don't even realize we're not singing along.

"It's all right, Marra. We would never have fit together back then. I needed to get away from here, find myself. You moved to Weaverville. Everyone went their own way and that was good. Now we've met again, and I like it that way."

He puts a finger under my chin and tilts my face so I can look at him again. Warmth and sincerity have found their way back into his gaze, causing warm butterflies to flutter in my stomach and making me smile softly. "Enjoying your time, baby?"

"Yes. What about you?"

He sighs and caresses my cheek. "You can't imagine how much I'm enjoying it."

I reach up to him and place my lips on his. Gently at first, then he holds me tight and presses us lovingly against each other. And there they are: The butterflies that shouldn't flutter. The fleeting thought of more, of a future that should disappear as quickly as it came. But my stupid body doesn't listen to my mind, instead it snuggles even closer to Jasper, as if we're a puzzle that's finally been solved.

"We're here," Lay says, and I disengage from Jasper. Valerian looks at us through the rear-view mirror, a sad expression in his eyes. But then he shakes his head, gets out and opens the door for me. He holds a hand out to me, which I gratefully accept and let him pull me out of the car.

When Jasper gets out, I see that he's carrying my bag and wearing my shoes, which makes me giggle softly. His white shirt is a little open and his hair is disheveled. With my shoes and bag, he looks like he's just committed a bank robbery in a boutique - or like he's the unwitting hero of a crazy romantic comedy.

And damn hot.

A strangled cry escapes my throat as Valerian throws me over his shoulder and my dress slips down my ass. My face dangles close to his tight ass and I laugh out loud as I clutch his hips with my hands. "Hey - what are you doing?"

Valerian gives me a good slap on the butt and I hear the other two laugh happily too. "We're going swimming, starlet."

Before I can contradict him, he runs off, a mixture of unbridled shouting and hearty laughter echoing through the forest from his throat. Out of the corner of my eye, I see Layton set our things down on the porch and then unbutton his shirt. Jasper takes off his clothes too.

The next second, all I feel is cold and wetness. The water surrounds me and my movements become sluggish as I try to swim to the surface. With kicking legs, I try to push myself up and as I break the surface, I gasp for air. My hair sticks to my cheeks, water runs down my face and I wipe my eyes before swimming in circles to check on Valerian.

He emerges and pulls his head back, flinging his hair out of his eyes. Slowly, his clothes come off his body. The shirt puffs out briefly before floating weightlessly to the surface.

There is a broad smile on his lips as he swims towards me. I bite my lower lip contentedly, wrap my arms around his neck and start planting kisses on his face and neck. "Oh, starlet, you're driving me crazy."

I don't tell him the feeling is mutual.

He slips the straps off my shoulders, reaches around my back to undo the cords and pull the dress off my body. My silk dress floats on the surface for a moment before being pulled into the depths. A soft giggle escapes me as I cling to him and we spin in the cool water, free from anything lurking on the shore.

Valerian tosses his shirt carelessly into the water and, as it is already soaked with water, it quickly sinks along with his suit trousers. Next he takes off my underwear, then his own boxer shorts.

"These fucking clothes," he growls as he finally gets everything off and I run my fingers over his hard chest. "I'll buy you a new dress and new underwear."

I shake my head silently, because even if he could afford it painlessly, I'd never want to ask him to do something like that. "It's just a scrap of cloth, Val," I assure him, licking his lips provocatively.

Jasper and Layton join us, also stark naked and with a wicked look on their faces. I pull away from Valerian and let myself fall onto my back a little, kicking my legs and enjoying the peace and quiet. Despite everything, I can feel their burning eyes on me.

Are they unable to simply enjoy the moment? The chirping birds and the warming sun, the feeling of peace?

Their hatred of Asheville, their childhood here and the stress of New York have polluted their souls. "Just let the peace carry you for a moment, boys."

Since I have my eyes closed, I can't see what they're doing, but they don't say anything back, so I assume they're listening to my advice.

I've never been skinny dipping before, but it's a pleasant and liberating feeling. And it seems like the boys can finally switch off properly. Normally I'd be sitting on the couch reading a book or taking care of Mrs. Jolly's order, which doesn't actually have to be ready for another three weeks. If I told my self from a week ago what I'm doing right now, I'd laugh at myself.

I giggle quietly to myself after dunking my head under water and surfacing again. The three men responsible for my good mood this weekend look at me with lively glances, causing me to bite my lip with a racing heart and look away in shame.

"Stop being embarrassed, little Mar." Layton grabs my hand under the water and pulls me towards him. Where he is, I can just barely touch the bottom with my feet, but before I can stand up properly, he reaches under my legs and lifts them up to buckle them around his waist. "Hey, slow down, young man."

He grins and strokes my spine until he gets to my bare ass and kneads it gently. "I'm not really ashamed," I admit and he tilts his head questioningly. His strawberry-blonde hair has grown longer due to the water and hangs in soft curls down his forehead. The amber of his eyes glows in the setting sun. He looks breathtakingly beautiful, and yet I know I won't have that forever.

"Then what is it?"

"It's unusual. I'm doing something for me and only me. Sure, you have a part in it too, but it's the first time I've broken out of my habit."

Lost in thought, I run my fingertip over his taut shoulders and the tense muscles of his arms. Drops of water roll off his skin and drip back into the lake. The sun makes the water glow orange and red, as if it had been created just for him. And the forest and grasses glow a lush green, as if these summer days were meant just for Jasper. The blue sky becomes darker and darker and more and more fascinating, as if Valerian's soul is trapped in it.

They all have a part of themselves here in Asheville, whether they like it or not. I see them in everything I have in front of me, they will always be there, even when they return to New York. I think that's what gives me comfort. This weekend will pass. But the memories will stay. They will show me that it's worth breaking the rules and enjoying life. They will prove to me that I can be different from what I've always convinced myself I can be.

Time is fleeting, but memories are infinite.

Suddenly, the warbling ring of a telephone pulls me from my thoughts and I hear Valerian cursing angrily as he wades through the water to his phone on the porch. "Work?" I ask Layton, who looks after Valerian with a monotone expression and shrugs his shoulders.

"Sì?" I hear Valerian humming into the phone, which makes me frown woundedly. "Who does he speak Italian with?"

Jasper sighs, shakes his head in disapproval and swims close to us. "Probably with a business partner. He speaks his father tongue a lot at work, didn't you know that?"

The three of us watch as he quickly dries himself off and hastily growls into the phone. "Domani pomeriggio prendo il volo per casa, non arrabiarti." Then he disappears into the house and leaves us alone. Satisfied, I lean my head back and Layton submerges me a little until the water touches my scalp. My breasts arch towards him and he takes the opportunity to gently bite and pull on my nipples.

A satisfied grin forms on my lips.

15
Some weed

Marra

He kisses his way down between my breasts, licks my skin again and again and bites it gently. Then he hugs me tightly to his chest, wades through the water and carries me as if I only weigh as much as a leaf. Over his shoulder, I can see Jasper, close on our heels. He smiles at me, his chest tense, but generally he finally seems a little happier.

As I look down, I see his cock twitch slightly and he gets even closer until he's level with Lay and me.

We walk across the lawn toward the porch, me still clinging to Layton like a fucking koala, until he sets me down on the lounge seat and sits at the other end. Jasper stops in front of me and puts a hand to my cheek, making me look up at him. I bite my lip excitedly and dig my fingers into the fabric of the outdoor couch as he strokes my cheek. Drops roll off our bodies and I follow their path with my eyes as they travel over his six-pack to his erect penis. Then he suddenly takes his hand away and nods in Layton's direction. I slide across the seats to him and sit unceremoniously on his lap. I place my hands flat on his chest and his find their way to my thighs. He looks at me. His eyes are intense and attentive, his lips open sensually, drops of water flowing over his skin. He slowly lifts his hand to my hair and strokes the wet strands back so that they flow down my bare back.

I draw small circles and shapes on his chest. "Touch me," I whisper. First he runs his hands up and down my arms, then he traces the contours of my face. With one hand on the back of my neck, he pulls me towards him and licks my lips. I close my eyes with pleasure and concentrate on his touch. His fingers move further down, circling my breasts and nipples, then he glides over my stomach and I shudder. This moment is more intimate than normal sex with them. I feel safe, embraced and loved.

"Does that feel good?" I nod in agreement and inhale shakily. Above all, it feels right. As if nothing that is yet to come in my life will be as right and certain as this moment here. I open my eyes flutteringly and meet his blazing gaze, which makes me groan. I lean forward.

I kiss him.

That's all I need at the moment. I want to feel him, want to taste him. He returns my kiss wildly and impatiently, thrusts his hips towards my crotch and touches my clit with his lust. He pushes me down, slides into me and I moan against his lips when he's all the way inside me. His fingers dig into my ass, our tongues circle each other, my fingers get lost in his hair and our skin sticks together wetly. I can feel Jasper's eyes on me, but he's already seen everything about me, already felt every part of my body.

I have nothing to be ashamed of.

Full of courage, I start to move on top of him and gyrate my hips. "God, Marra, I could do this forever." Our lips hover close together as I now move up and down, feeling his cock slide in and out again and again. The friction does something to me - brings me to a point where I lose myself. My heart opens up, almost bursting with excitement. I couldn't even put into words how important these men have become to me if I took a week to do it. No words in all 7,000 languages of these 193 countries in our world could describe the feeling that is in my chest and makes my heart beat faster. It is hard to comprehend.

I've been with these men for less than 48 hours and it already feels like they've turned my world upside down.

I'm not talking about earth-shattering feelings here - but I am talking about a sudden self-confidence, a sense of well-being, a sense of protection that I've never felt before. This is like coming home.

And suddenly, for a split second, there's the thought that I've been dreading all this time.

What if I go with them? Start a life in New York?

It would be a life full of passion, a life between three men I really like. I don't have to marry any of them.

I'm not the kind of woman who spends her whole life waiting for her dream wedding anyway. I plan the decorations for such events, but I'm never on the guest list and I'm not the person who performs the ceremony. I could be living in the shadows of New York, in their penthouse, flitting between their beds. I could make them breakfast, let them relax after a long day at work. Leo could sweeten their man pad a little.

These thoughts don't fit in at all with what we've agreed. We each needed a break. But what if we're just not happy with our lives anymore and need that to be able to breathe again? And not just for a weekend.

But is that what they want? Surely not.

They're relying on our deal.

At least Jasper and Layton are, I'm not so sure about Valerian.

Suddenly, two other hands grab me and drag me out of the sphere I've created for myself. Brutally torn from my thoughts, I look around in confusion and only see a hint of Jasper before he puts me on all fours on the lounge seat and stands behind me. I feel him push himself between my buttocks, then he penetrates me deeply and animalistically. I lower my head with a moan. I'm wet, but tight, damn tight.

"Yes," I gasp as he runs a hand down to my clit and gently strokes and plays with my pearl. "You look so beautiful, baby." My heart is beating incredibly fast and my hands are starting to sweat. I awkwardly wipe them on the fabric.

He pulls back and then thrusts into me even harder. He finds the rhythm, does it again and again, sometimes softer, sometimes harder and I moan in the most beautiful tones.

"Valerian should paint a picture of this, for fuck's sake. It would look much better in our apartment than these fucking cloud paintings," I hear Layton say and smile to myself. Stunned, I lift my head and look around for him and find him right next to me. He's rolled himself a joint, where he suddenly got the stuff for it - no idea, but he lights it and puts it between his lips before taking a light drag and winking at me. "You want some, little one?"

I lick my lips, trying to ignore the bouncing of my breasts and focus my brain. Just for a few seconds. But Jasper robs me of all my sanity, all my being, as he fucks me like there's nothing he'd rather be doing than this. He leans forward, pushes deep inside me and bites my back. It's a magical feeling, engaging and somehow indestructible. As he leans back again, he lets his palm slam against my plump ass.

I let out a hissing breath, my knees buckle a little and I want to groan out loud, but Layton suddenly holds the joint in front of my lips and I clutch it. Without hesitating any longer, I take a drag and inhale deeply before closing my eyes and feeling the rush running through my body. A tingling sensation wets my entire skin, my thoughts disappear between the clouds and I take a second drag. "Don't overdo it, little one. You're not used to this."

But I don't listen to him and inhale the stuff like it's a fucking asthma inhaler. He pulls the joint away again and hands it to Jasper, who strokes my back supportively, moving slower inside me by now, probably to give me a breather. As he pulls on the joint, his prominent jaw tenses and I watch him closely as he moves.

"This is just like old times," I mumble, and Layton laughs raucously. Shortly after my fifteenth birthday, he rolled me my first joint of three so far. Well, now it's four. "Better, little one. It's a thousand times better than before."

I'm about to come, which isn't just because of the fog in my head, but because of the wave of feelings that suddenly floods me. I could swear that my juices are already running down my thighs.

Gasping, I tense my pelvic floor muscles. Now Jasper moans deep and loud, interrupting his movements and running his fingers over my ass. "Damn, baby."

I grin and turn my gaze away again.

He seems to like it, even though I don't really know what I'm doing. But I can feel his hands all over me. It's as if he wants his fingertips to imprint every inch of my skin. My thighs tremble and my bottom aches but I don't care, I let Jasper continue to slide inside me. I circle my head with pleasure and claw even harder into the pillows. Layton is smoking pot and blowing smoke in my face, which makes me cough slightly, but I quickly catch myself.

But then Jasper pulls out of me and squirts on my back. "You've made me too horny," he murmurs close to my ear and I shudder at his words. I sit down carefully on my ass and the next moment I feel Jasper wiping the cum off my back with a towel. Layton is still watching us with a grin and I snuggle up close to him, he puts an arm protectively around my shoulders and presses a kiss to my temple.

"We're not done here yet, little Mar. Don't rest too much."

I giggle and lavish kisses on his bare chest until I get to his private parts and lick over his length. With one hand, I reach for his balls, kneading them gently as I continue to play with my tongue. As I turn my eyes up to him, I see him frown, his eyes slightly red-rimmed and his lips sensually parted. It continues like this until I finally swallow Lay's cum, come once more on Jasper's tongue and then stretch out wide on the couch.

But it's the moment when Layton lays his head on my chest and dozes off that makes my chest tighten. Layton doesn't sleep around other people. And yet he does, in my arms. Pride and joy flow through me at the realization that he must trust me a lot. Because Jasper keeps looking at us in surprise too, as if he can't believe what he sees in front of him. "Wait a minute," he says and then jumps up, disappears into the hut and returns a few moments later. He has a digital camera in his hand, which he now points at us. "Don't worry, his thick skull covers everything that should be covered." He winks at me and I giggle, but quickly refrain as Layton grumbles deeply. Putting a finger to my lips, I look at Jas, who just rolls his eyes exaggeratedly.

And it's a fantastic moment.

16

Bambi

Layton

The sun burns pleasantly on my skin as I lie on the picnic blanket and fold my arms behind my head. Marra and Jasper are lying together in a deckchair on the veranda, her face nestled against his warm chest, and she seems to have dozed off.

Still a little dazed, I look at her. I've fallen asleep on her - which never happens at all. Never with anyone. But she left me there, stayed awake until I eventually regained my wits and escaped onto this picnic blanket. Now she's the one resting.

Her bare feet dangle over the edge and she's wearing a white summer dress. Jasper is lovingly stroking her light brown hair, and she has one of those innocent, relaxed expressions on her face as she sleeps, her body thinking that no one is watching her. Jasper whispers something quietly to her that neither she nor I can understand. I haven't seen him this gentle and compassionate in a long time. He cares about her, it's important to him that she's okay, and he hasn't had a steady girlfriend since he broke up with Jadie. He has gotten what he needed, but he has never cared for any of his nightly visitors.

But the look he gives Marra - I haven't seen that look on him for a long time. Valerian lets himself fall onto the picnic blanket next to me with a sigh and stretches his face towards the sun, lying on his back and putting an arm over his face.

"What did she want?"

He sighs deeply and shakes his head silently.

Not now - I understand the gesture.

We have a life in New York that we have to return to because we have no other choice. We have to do our job, the company is our greatest treasure. But that's not all: in Valerian's projects, Jasper and I are like his right-hand men. We're not one hundred percent involved, but we help him with his business with Klaus Diabolus. Ever since Valerian heard about him as a fourteen-year-old boy, he knew that once he realized that Klaus was his ticket out, he would do anything to escape his personal nightmare.

His stepfather broke Valerian, and his mother did nothing about it. Val lost everything, even himself, until he became successful with our company in New York. In the beginning, we lived in a shabby old shared flat, took out a big loan and accumulated a lot of debt. It wasn't just sleepless nights, but years. Then our success grew, our company became better known because Jasper had the perfect idea. Enough people became aware of it - including Klaus. Since then, the two have been in contact, closing deals and projects, and Valerian has almost achieved what he always wanted.

To be seen without being the center of attention.

To have power and money without fear of it being taken away from him.

A family, even if it is not related by blood, but we are with him and would never leave his side.

Marra is an important piece of the puzzle in Valerian's checklist, I realize that at least as much as Jasper. We've all dreamed of her, longed for her. But Valerian coveted her and hurt himself when he turned his back on her. As a little boy, he was a lot like Marra. He put himself last until he had to learn early on that he wouldn't get far that way. If he had continued to care more about others than himself back then, he would be dead now.

But there was a part of him that Marra never forgot.

He didn't let on, but Jas and I aren't stupid. We thought about her too, we missed her. But Valerian longed for her, his soul was searching for a way back to her.

"Klaus is coming to New York next week."

I look at him, see the toughness he has acquired over the last few years to unsettle his clients. "It'll all work out, Val. Enjoy your last few hours here." He nods and rubs his face.

"OH MY GOD." Marra sits down on Jasper's lap and rubs her tight ass against his crotch. She looks at us excitedly.

"Whoa girl, if you move like that again, I'll fuck you here and now," Jasper grumbles and grabs her ass. Valerian and I laugh as Marra gives him a dirty look and then points in the direction where she must have spotted something. When I look there too, I know why she's so pleased.

A small fawn stands at the edge of the forest, still a little wobbly on its thin legs, and looks curiously in our direction. The warm sunlight makes its fur shine. "It's so cute," I hear Marra whisper softly to Jasper, who is obviously still busy concentrating on something other than her bottom.

She almost trips over her own feet as she walks towards the clearing. Jas lets his fingers slip from her before leaning forward and running a hand over his face. Today has been a difficult day for him and enough crazy things have happened to distract him. But nothing distracts him like Marra does. He watches her as she carefully leaves the porch with velvet-footed, light steps. She approaches the deer quietly, but stays far enough away not to scare it away. Then she crouches down, leans back and rests her arms on the grass. There is a broad, beautiful smile on her lips.

Valerian grunts next to me. "Oh no, not more animals. She's already got that damn cat."

I grin. "And now another deer? Maybe she'll move to a petting zoo soon."

Jasper lifts his digital camera and takes a photo. But not with the fawn in focus, but of Marra looking at the animal with beaming eyes. Then he lowers them again and murmurs almost tenderly: "My Bambi."

I snort in amusement, but Marra is far too fascinated by her new forest friend to hear us.

"Did you know that deer in the wild often..." Valerian raises his hand defensively, not bothering to open his eyes. "Starlet. I love you, but I'm not going to listen to facts about deer right now."

I love you?

I look at him, dumbfounded.

Jasper laughs. "I think it's a perfect fit. Shy, gentle, big brown eyes - she's just like the fawn." Like me, Marra looks in amazement at Valerian, who grins mischievously. Then he raises his eyebrows as if to say, *"What, you don't think I have feelings?"* But I hope Marra doesn't take his words too seriously.

Val agrees with Jasper. "And if you scare her or say something that shocks her, she'll jump away just as panicked." Marra's face hardens as she seems to recognize the provocation and innuendo. She straightens up, clicks her tongue and puts her hands on her hips. "Very funny."

"No, really now," he continues, this time with a serious expression on his face, designed to annoy her even more. "You're our little Bambi. Fragile. Sensitive. You need your quiet forest to feel safe."

The deer startles at his loud voice, turns and runs back into the forest, tempting Marra to burn poisoned arrows into its head. I join in the game. "As if she could ever do anything that ..." I gesture vaguely. "Well. Risky."

She squints her eyes. I can almost see it rattling and glowing behind her forehead. She doesn't like us talking about her like this.

But it's fun to tease her a little.

"Oh yeah?"

"Yeah." Valerian grins and closes his eyes again. In the light of the setting sun, his hair looks almost golden and his skin glows. "If you want to prove me wrong, please do."

There is silence for a second. Jasper and I look at our little girl, but she just stares angrily at Valerian.

Then suddenly - she starts moving. Marra turns and runs quickly across the grass - straight towards our bikes.

"Oh, shit." I straighten up, take a step towards her. The keys are in the ignition.

"She doesn't dare," Val says, but I still notice his nonchalance slowly disappearing. "Baby, don't do anything stupid!" Jas calls after her.

But she doesn't hesitate for a second. She swings herself onto the bike, her fingers clutching the handlebars, and before either of us can react, she starts the thing. The engine roars. Jasper starts laughing. "That woman will drive me to my grave."

"Marra!" shouts Valerian. "You can't be serious!" But she only half-turns towards us, raises her hand with a grin - and accelerates. Then she's gone. All that remains is the dust on the road, Valerian's incredulous swearing, Jasper's clapping and my satisfied grin.

17

The fire wins

Marra

My heart is still pounding rapidly against my ribs and the wind is blowing through my hair as I switch off the engine and take a deep breath. I feel a mixture of adrenaline, euphoria and fear rushing through my veins - an untamed and completely unfamiliar energy that completely overwhelms me.

I have gone mad.

I've stolen Valerian's motorcycle.

And I'm still alive.

The dark clapping behind me catches my attention. I turn around and see Valerian coming towards me. His posture is casual, almost provocative, but his blue eyes sparkle. Perhaps with amusement, perhaps with pure amazement. But with a hint of recognition.

He shakes his head slowly. "You stole my fucking bike, Marra." His voice is low and calm - far too calm. It reminds me a little of the old school days, and that's not a good sign. Back then, he was always cold - he didn't care about anything. He was the same to everyone.

But I don't let this bad feeling get to me. I jut my chin, cross my arms in front of my chest and reply coolly: "And you said I was like a deer." I shrug my shoulders. "Deer don't steal motorcycles." Layton, who is standing a few steps away, bursts out laughing. Jasper, who has been watching the scene skeptically, runs his fingers through his hair in amusement, but I can clearly see something in his eyes: Pride.

"The point goes to her."

Val looks at me in silence for a moment. Then the corners of his mouth twist into an amused smile. "Or she's just damn lucky she didn't end up in a crash barrier."

"There are no crash barriers here. Just trees," I remark and he raises his right eyebrow provocatively. "Which would you prefer, yellow star?"

I shrug my shoulders again. I'm not sure what I was expecting - for them to laugh at me or tell me I'm being irresponsible. But instead they are silent. And it's in that silence that I feel it: the freedom and the numbing feeling still coursing through my veins. I have done something that I thought was impossible. But that's exactly what this weekend is all about.

And it feels damn good, it's true.

I have a gratitude inside me that the boys can't even imagine. They have given me this freedom. They've given me feelings that actually matter to me and that I'm not afraid of. Well - not directly.

But as the adrenaline slowly wears off, I can feel the exhaustion in my limbs. The tiredness that mixes with the approaching evening chill. I take off my clothes, leaving me in just my underwear. Many years ago, my father attached a swing to the sturdy branch of a tree that towers over the lake. As a child, it was my absolute favorite retreat. I quickly scurry into the house, go up to my room and find a book from the shelf next to my bed.

Leaving the boys behind, I wade over to the old swing and then push myself off the bottom of the lake to pull myself up by the ropes,

"Do you want to play a round?" Valerian calls to me, but I just shake my head as I look over my shoulder at them. "No, thanks. Play without me..."

They undress, but this time they leave their boxers on, much to my regret, and then jump into the water. There's a beach ball under Jasper's arms, which he throws to Val shortly afterwards. I turn away, take a few deep breaths and soak up the energy of nature. I close my eyes for a moment and let my mind wander.

I think I am completely out of my mind.

The wind gently caresses my skin, the evening sun bathes the leaves in warm gold.

My feet dangle in the water up to my calves. Satisfied, I open the book and read a little. It's the story of a little boy who is separated from his parents and grows up with his uncle in an old villa. I'm caught up in the little boy's everyday

life and the intrigues that unfold when I suddenly see Layton swimming towards me.

"Still processing your little outburst, Speed Queen?" Lay's voice is calm, warm - a contrast to the slight smirk he wears on his lips. His honey-blonde hair is slightly tousled and he stands close to me.

"Maybe." He gives me a gentle push and I let myself rock gently back and forth. He looks at me for a moment. "So, how was it?"

I think about it and look down at my feet. "Scary. But also..." I pause and search for the right word. "Liberating."

"Liberating, huh?" He raises an eyebrow. "Maybe there's more to you than just the shy little deer after all."

I laugh softly and shake my head. "Or maybe the deer just learned that it can run."

Layton looks at me, his gaze softening for a moment. I don't know what he's thinking, but I can feel it - this unspoken understanding that lies between us. A bond that feels like it's always been there. As if he's always seen me like this.

It's quiet for a few heartbeats. Just the laughter of the boys still frolicking on the shore.

Then he looks at me. Not like before. Different. He looks as if he doesn't know how to start. It's a moment when you know something is coming. Something big.

"I missed you," he says quietly.

"You could have written."

"You too."

Touché.

He gives me a soft smile and then looks out at the water. "I was never quite sure back then if you saw me the way I saw you," he murmurs and I look at him. My heart leaps dangerously, head first into the deep water - on the verge of drowning. His hands are clasped together. "I was the buddy. The one who brought you home at night when the others wanted to party on. The one who misbehaved to make you laugh." He shakes his head. "You were my safe place, Marra. You and me - that was easy. And I fucked up because I thought we'd be better off not touching it."

I laugh softly and it's a sad, tender sound. "And what do you think now?"

"You're here now, and this doesn't feel like high school anymore." He swallows and I take a deep breath. I understand his language, hear every single word, but I struggle to form a thought that can give him an answer.

I remember so many moments from our youth. How we lay together on his balcony, paying the stars, our fingers almost touching, but never quite.

"The deal was that this weekend would end. That you would go back. And me too. I don't want to say anything because I don't want you to leave and go home feeling like I'm... hoping for something."

"But you're hoping?"

He grins crookedly. "Maybe a little."

His gaze softens and he gently grabs my knees. "You know, the falling asleep in your arms thing... I don't do that. I can't sleep when someone is that close but with you it was suddenly so natural. Not easy but somehow not hard either."

I swallow hard. There's a nasty feeling in my throat that I can't get rid of. I wish I could say more, say more in response, but my mind is bordering on insanity. I'm incredibly confused and unsure - don't know if there's even a right decision.

Layton dips his head under the water and closes his eyes. "You know I'll stay if that's what you want, right? I'll go anywhere with you. The boys and the company wouldn't matter. Just... you would matter."

I turn slightly to the side, looking at his profile. The twitch of his lips, like he regrets what he just said. "You guys are like family," I interject, and he grimaces in agony. "Even family members choose different paths sooner or later. But they still remain a family." I lick my lips nervously. "And what if I myself don't know what and where I want to go?" I ask quietly. He opens his eyes and looks at me silently for a few seconds. "Then I'll stay until you know." It feels like there's a bomb in my chest, radiating heat, ready to explode at any moment.

I gather my courage and finally close the book on my lap. "What if I come with you?" He looks at me, calm and collected, thinking carefully about his next words.

"Then I'll pretend it was your plan. And not mine for years." I giggle softly but feel the conversation tighten around my throat like a noose. I don't know if I should make jokes. Whether I should reveal all my thoughts to him. But the look he doesn't give me makes me feel like I should be honest.

"Why did you never say anything to me before?" His voice becomes deeper, calmer.

"I could live with just being a friend. But I couldn't have stood it if you'd suddenly turned your back on me completely." That's the problem with Layton. He doesn't speak often - rarely emotionally. But when he does, it lands right between the ribs.

Sighing, I look away.

"I always thought you only stayed because you had to," I whisper. He shakes his head abruptly. "I'm staying because I want to. I never saw you as any kind of option. You were always the one I was waiting for, without really realizing it myself."

Silence.

Seconds pass that drag on like minutes.

Then: "Whoa, that was too much, wasn't it?"

I grin. "Maybe a little. But in a way that won't be forgotten."

There is something in his gaze that has finally dared to emerge from the darkness. I lift my hand and place it gently against his cheek. My forehead is furrowed and I look at his entire face. From the wavy strands of hair, to the sparkling eyes and snub nose, to his full lips. "I don't know how this is going to end."

"Neither do I," he replies. "But I'd love to be there when it starts."

I search for an answer in his amber eyes, a solution to all my problems. I search for the end of the thread that will untie the knot. "I have no idea what's right, Lay." He doesn't answer right away, giving me space to breathe. Just like before. Like always.

"You don't have to make a decision now either," he says. "Not today. Not tomorrow. Maybe not until we're long back in New York."

Once again, I imagine life in New York. What my everyday life would be like. But there's not much I can imagine. I don't know how things work there. I don't know a big city, I've never left this side of North Carolina. But they warned me about themselves. Tried to tell me several times that my life didn't fit in with theirs. Not for a long time.

But I wish so much that it were different.

Tears sting my eyes but I can feel his fingers tracing soothing circles over my knees.

"You know I can feel it, don't you?" I finally ask him. "You. Them. Everything." My voice is high and shaky.

Layton looks at me for longer than he should and then nods curtly. "Yes, little girl. But I think you need to find out if you can still feel yourself. Do what's right for you, not what we want you to do." Then he removes his fingers, swims a little away from me and smiles at me. "Don't worry about it, little Mar. There is no perfect decision. Just the ones that let you sleep well at night." This sentence echoes through my head. It is so honest that it touches me deeply. And maybe that's all I can take.

"I never asked you how you felt back then because I thought it was enough if I knew." I wipe away a single tear that has started its way down my cheek and press my lips together. I nod.

"And I never said I let you go to New York, even though I didn't want to."

"I thought I'd just have to leave one day and give you the chance to build your own life the way you really want to. And I still want that, little Mar." There is tenderness, sincerity and a hint of sadness in his gaze that tears at my heart. Then his expression changes and he nods bravely at me.

I smile brokenly. He turns away. Back to the shore. Back to the boys. Back to New York, soon at least. I stay sitting on the swing, looking at the water glistening in the light.

Three men. Three paths. And me in the middle.

Maybe I'm not a deer that runs after all.

Maybe I'm just someone who stops when everyone else keeps going.

But then he turns to me one last time while Jasper pushes the rusty grill in front of the hut and Valerian gives him strict instructions. Lay raises his hand to his mouth and shouts: "One thing's for sure: riding a motorcycle barefoot and only in a dress? Bloody hot."

A few hours later, I'm still grinning at his words. Even funnier, however, is his and Jasper's pitiful attempt to make a fire. There's still a plate of leftovers from our barbecue on my lap - the boys really let off steam at the grill and felt like real men. Jasper even thought the pink apron was really cool and Layton had one with flames on it. Only Val looked a bit silly with the unicorns, but I didn't tell him that. Of course not.

Now he can enjoy watching Jas and Lay make fools of themselves while he sits relaxed next to me, watching his boys with an indifferent expression. "How was that? You guys are super knowledgeable about nature?" I tease them and Layton gives me the middle finger. "Have faith in us, baby. It's about to burst into flames."

Valerian rolls his eyes at Jasper's words. "The only thing that's about to go up in flames is my cigarette." He takes one out of the pack and puts it between his lips. The crackling of wood hitting stone and Jasper's quiet cursing distract me from continuing to watch him closely. "Are you kidding me, bro? It can't be that hard, can it?" Layton snatches the tool from Jasper and pushes him a little to the side, making me laugh out loud. My stomach is full, I'm stuffed to the brim and satisfied. And these two idiots are my evening program.

We've settled down on picnic blankets in front of the hut, wrapped ourselves in woollen blankets and collected wood that we actually wanted to use for a campfire. "People have been making fires for centuries," Lay grumbles and Jas blows into the small flame, which flickers briefly - and then goes out again. "I'm telling you, the wood is damp."

"Or you're just incompetent," Valerian's amused voice sounds next to me, where he leans back with a beer in his hand. The cigarette is half smoked.

Layton and Jasper exchange an annoyed look. "Do better, Blondie," Jas finally growls, throwing wood and stones at Val, but he just gives them the cold shoulder. "I'm not going to make an ass of myself like you. Two alpha males against a fire - and the fire wins." I laugh and Layton gives me a dirty look.

Valerian stands up calmly, walks towards the fire with an exaggeratedly casual movement and reaches into the pocket of his jeans - and pulls out his lighter. Without another word, he holds it up to the fire, turns the wheel and seconds later small flames flicker out.

Silence.

"Asshole." Layton throws a piece of wood at him. "That's not fair."

"Smarter thinking, bro."

I chuckle and pull the blanket tighter around my shoulders. The fire crackles softly, casting warm shadows on our faces as the sky above us sinks into dark blue.

Val sits down next to me and holds his beer in front of me. I take a sip with relish and snuggle up to him.

I enjoy the moment.

The feeling of not being alone.

To be with them and, perhaps for the first time in my life, to be seen for who I really am. They want and accept me. And the worst thing they can do, but haven't done from the start: They don't go easy on me. They give me the full program.

I have people with me to keep me company and I feel good enough for the first time. It's worth it.

I am worth it.

I look into the flames. And suddenly there's that thought again, that crazy thought buzzing around in my head.

What if I went to New York with them?

What if I just do it?

What the hell?

As I lift my head, I meet Jasper's gaze. He looks at me like he knows exactly what's going on inside me.

But I don't tell him.

Because Layton said I should be able to sleep peacefully with my decision. Can I do that? Would a life in New York be peaceful?

I don't tell him.

Because as much as I'm enjoying this moment - as much as it feels like home - I know it can't last.

That's the deal.

18
Competition without a jury

Valerian

Oh, this is going to be great," I say with a grin as I pull an old canvas out of the dusty box. "I can't wait to beat you, starlet." She rolls her eyes and blows a strand of light brown hair out of her face. She sits on the dilapidated chest of drawers, her hands under her thighs, her hair pinned up with a barrette.

While the others were still sitting outside by the fire, I explored the house and made a great discovery. Then I made her put on old clothes and push her hair out of her face.

"I haven't painted for years. They might have been here since the last time I needed them for school," she tries to defend herself, but I shake my head. "Perfect. Then the chance of winning is even greater."

I look at the dried paint stains on the old wooden floor of the storeroom, then at the dented shelf with a few unopened pots of paint. Everything looks as if it's only here because it's been waiting for this moment.

I carry everything from the storage room into the living room, where I've covered the entire floor with a plastic sheet. Jasper and Layton are sitting on the couch, watching us with amused looks and eating the leftovers from the barbecue. "Are you guys having an art battle or what?" Layton asks, taking a sip of his beer. Marra finally comes into the room too, arms crossed in front of her chest, looking at me like I'm tired of living. But I'm not. I want us to enjoy the last few hours of this weekend.

And to the full.

I don't want to regret it. I want to make the most of everything and seize every opportunity for fun and freedom that comes our way.

I take the first pot of paint - bright blue - and open it with a loud crack "That's exactly what we're doing."

Marra snorts and raises an eyebrow. But there's so much emotion and affection in her eyes for me that I know she's joking. She's always loved the slightly artificial side of me. And she likes me far too much not to join in now.

There's so much love, tenderness and passion in her eyes and in her body language that I just want to go down on her. But first I want to win. "And how exactly are you going to judge that? We don't have a jury."

"We can do that." Jasper raises his left hand helpfully in the air, but Marra waves it away. "You don't know anything about art. You judge by sympathy." Jasper looks at her indignantly. "I think that's a brazen and vile lie. Did you hear that, Lay? She doesn't trust us to do the job well."

Lay shakes his head in agreement and looks at Marra with his lips pressed together. "You're hitting us right in the heart, Mar."

She laughs and throws both boys a kissing hand before turning back to me. I wipe some paint off my lid with two fingers and grin. "Oh, I don't need a jury. I already know I'm going to win."

She looks at me challengingly. "Oh yeah, you cocky snob?"

"Yeah."

And before she can answer, I pull my hand back and stroke her cheek with the blue paint. She freezes for a moment and inhales sharply. Then I see it - the sparkle in her eyes.

"You. Did. Not."

I laugh and turn to grab another pot of paint, but she's quicker. Before I can even come close to reacting or dodging, I feel something cold on the back of my neck.

"Damn it, starlet!" I run my hand over the spot and then look at the yellow color. Oh.

"I guess leaving yellow paint on my canvas eight years ago wasn't enough for you. Are you going to turn me into a yellow, glowing star now too?" She purses her lips mockingly and looks at me triumphantly. "The only star here is me."

I laugh out loud as my heart skips a beat at this statement.

Then she points to my chest and I look down. There, too, yellow streaks adorn my skin. "Maybe you're not so invincible after all."

"Don't get any ideas, starlet." I reach for another pot - red. In a flash, I dip my hand in it and stroke her breast. She shrieks and tries to flee backwards, but I hold her tight, my fingers dipped in paint as they glide over her arms.

Her skin is warm under my hands from all the sun she's gotten today, and for a moment I almost forget it's a game.

Jasper and Layton have long since taken cover, the cowards have fled the field of fire, but they keep cheering us on. "Come on, Marra! Show him where the paintbrush hangs!"

The canvas lies on the floor, long forgotten, while we paint each other and become a human canvas ourselves. Marra is breathing heavily, her cheeks are flushed. "Okay, okay! Stop!"

She raises her hands. "We're even."

I look at her. Her bright yellow blends with my blue and the red on her chest. Our fingerprints and handprints are all over our arms, shoulders and faces. Not to mention our tops.

Suddenly I realize how close we are. Her chest rises and falls quickly, as if she's run a marathon, and I'm sure it's not just from our little game. She is just as aware of our closeness as I am. My eyes catch the red stripes on her collarbone, stretching across her shoulder to the top of her shirt. My body reacts faster than my mind and my cock pushes hard against my pants.

"Oh fuck," I growl, grabbing her wrist to pull her closer to me. "I don't think we're quite done yet." Her gaze flickers - lust, curiosity and greed in it.

I want to know what she tastes like with all that color.

I want to know if she melts under my hands the same way the color melts on her skin.

With a jerk, I lean forward, determined to conquer her mouth. It's exactly as it should be - wild, uncontrolled, as if it's long overdue.

My hands glide over her waist, over the paint that feels warm and sticky as I press her against the easel and her own canvas. Her fingers run through my hair, leaving blue and yellow trails, but I don't care.

Moaning, I slide a leg between her and pull her shirt over her head as she bites my lip, wanting more, and then lets it pop out of her mouth.

We lose ourselves in that moment. In the heat. In the chaos of colors, skin, passion and desire.

When we finally break away from each other, she is breathless, her lips are swollen, and the canvas behind her - the only thing not yet covered in paint - is now a single work of art made of blue, red, yellow and all the colors that have blended through our touch. They show a work of art that none of us planned.

A work of art that was created by just the two of us.

I look at her and grin. "I'd say I've won."

She laughs softly, her fingers sliding onto my chest, "I think it's a tie."

I lean in closer, my forehead against hers, "I guess we'll have to have a rematch then."

She returns my grin. "Maybe."

Jas and Lay, who have taken cover in the meantime, look at us with satisfaction. "So...," Lay begins slowly. "I hope for your sake the paint isn't toxic."

Jasper shakes his head in amusement. "I knew it would escalate."

Marra giggles, her forehead still leaning against mine. And in that moment, I realize I'll never get enough of her. I want to have her with me for the rest of my life, because maybe what I said to her before her motorcycle outburst wasn't just pure provocation. Maybe a part of me really loves her. Maybe not a very big one, but if I trust the feeling in my chest, that part is getting bigger by every minute.

With nimble fingers, she unzips my pants and lets them fall down.

This action makes me so horny that I have to take a deep breath. I like it when she knows what she wants. Don't talk too much about it, just do it. I like it when she dares.

She takes off her own pants and goes to the paint pots, then turns to the other two. "Take off your clothes." As if stung by a tarantula, they do as my little star tells them and throw their clothes carelessly across the room. I take off all my clothes too and wait for my next command. Jas and Lay stand close to me as if to salute.

Mar looks at us with a mischievous grin, then takes a paintbrush and dips it in the blue paint.

"Now let's really get going."

She stands in front of me first, lifts the brush to my forehead and looks intently at the area of skin she wants to paint. The paint is cold on my skin but all I have my head for is this sexy woman in front of me.

I can feel it.

Her gaze.

The love and passion she puts into her delicate movements. When she's finished with my forehead, she tilts her head with a grin and places the tip of the brush on my hip. I want to look down, but she shakes her head sternly. "Na-na, Val. Not until everyone's finished." I nod in agreement and let her finish her work. She draws something on Layton's shoulders, but I don't dare turn my head in his direction to get a better look. In the end, she throws a full pot at my skull. She applies the brush to Jasper's chest, then turns him around and paints something on his ass. Curiosity flares up in me and I can hardly stand still.

She takes a few steps back and looks at her work - a cynical smile on her lips. Then she bursts out laughing. "I think it's all very accurate." I finally turn my head towards my best friends. I narrow my eyes, trying to make out everything. The one on Jasper's chest is most definitely a barcode. A barcode? What the hell does that mean? I stretch my neck to look at his butt and have to snort. It's a smiley face. Layton, on the other hand, has eyes painted on both shoulder blades, with an infinity sign underneath. Then I look down at myself and pause.

She's not serious.

"Don't forget where your ego is," she laughs and I cross my arms in front of my chest. She has drawn an arrow in the direction of my cock - the little witch. "And what's on my forehead?"

Lay and Jas take a look and raise their eyebrows. "I guess a... halo?" Perplexed, I look at Jasper.

"Why is that?" I ask and Marra approaches me, pleased. She wraps her arms around my neck, stands on tiptoe and hovers her lips close to mine as she whispers: "A man with so many sins needs at least a little compensation."

Oh - if only she knew.

Emotionally, she lets our lips melt together and I return the kiss, happy that she's at least having fun. "Uh, but wait a minute. What's with our signs?" Layton rubs the back of his neck in embarrassment and Marra slowly pulls away from me and stands in front of them with her arms crossed. "The smiley face on his butt? So everyone knows how happy Jas feels in that area." She winks at Jas, but then raises a hand to her lips and whispers to Lay, "I think he likes butts."

Jas laughs harshly. "Damn right you guessed it, baby."

She shrugs. "The barcode is just in case someone wants to return you. Or buy you. Or both."

The smile on his lips slips and he scowls at her. But before he can close back, Marra is already moving on to Layton. "The eyes are for seeing when you run away from your feelings again. The infinity sign for your everlasting loyalty and support." She then walks towards them both, leaps dangerously into their arms and then ends up in a hug, being crushed from both sides. Smiling silently, I wait.

After a few seconds, I grab her hand and pull her towards me on the couch. The foil crackles softly, the room is bathed in subdued light - only the floor lamp next to the fireplace is lit. Jasper is still staring at her scrutinizingly.

"Why are you looking at me like that?" she asks.

"How am I looking?" Jas teases, his gaze traveling from her eyes down to her lips.

"Like you want to eat me."

I see her swallow hard and rub her hands against her thighs. "What if I do?" He moves closer, kneels on the floor in front of Marra and runs his hand up her inner thigh. She bites her lip, trying to ignore his touch, but her physical reaction doesn't escape me. Her nipples stand up and her cheeks flush slightly.

"Then I would ask you how hungry you are." She should stop provoking him, otherwise this could get very, very messy very quickly. To save her from that, I reach for her face, turn it towards me and place my lips on hers again. My tongue slides in and she moans a little, my teeth linger on her tongue. I tease her, put my hands on her hips and run them up and down. In the background, I can hear Jasper lighting a cigarette and leaning against the wall, watching us and paying attention to every little movement. She's whimpering and I realize that this sound isn't just my fault, so I gently pull away from her. Layton has spread her thighs, face lowered to her center, his nose sliding up her slit. Her cheeks are turning bright pink but I won't allow her to find this uncomfortable for a second.

I'd rather drown in that lake out there.

"Layton..." He interrupts her pleading and licks his tongue, then draws in a circular motion. Jasper joins us with the cigarette in his mouth, wraps a hand around Marra's bare breast and strokes her nipple. Then he takes the cigarette between his other fingers and closes his lips around her nipple. I take the cigarette from him so that he can twist the other nipple with his other hand while Layton conquers her pussy.

Suddenly her hand moves to the back of my neck and pulls me towards her again. She presses her lips to mine stormily, burying her fingers firmly in my hair.

My cock is throbbing, erect and ready for more. I want everything. Everything she can offer and give me.

I take my cock in my hand, stroke myself and lose all sense of space and time. I don't want it to ever end. Our tongues circle each other, she bites my lip every now and then until I feel my own blood, and she only gasps for breath before she pounces on me again. Layton goes wild too, spreading her even wider, biting her tender skin and she gasps under my kiss. Jasper alternates between her breasts, kneading and twirling, licking and sucking.

Then Layton pulls her closer, making her cry out in surprise, and rubs her pussy against his cock. "Which one do you want first?" he asks. Her eyes shoot to him, her eyelashes fluttering. His lips are smeared with her wetness, as if he's wearing a gloss, and his eyes gleam with satisfaction. Meanwhile, Jasper lets his hand wander over her belly, down to her pearl and rubs it.

I can see that she wants to give him an answer, but she's so aroused and taken with Jasper's hand play that her chin trembles slightly and she wrinkles her forehead. I bet she can't think a decent thought right now.

Then he slides his fingers inside her, she slumps a little but Layton holds her securely. Our bodies are still smeared with the paint. Colorful splotches of paint stretch all over our skin, blending together and forming a new color palette.

"Oh my God," she moans, throwing her head back.

Her eyes are closed as Jasper rhythmically moves his fingers into hers, bending her until she arches her back and gasps for air. Then he pulls it out and holds it in front of her lips. "Taste." She willingly opens her mouth and tastes her own sweetness. Excited, I squeeze my cock tighter and then pull her away from them. "I want to do this forever," I hear Jasper say, and I want to tell him that this could be the last time.

But this realization hits me hard too.

It could be the last time we are this close. Only a few more hours before we fly back to New York. I know she had a conversation with Layton earlier. About what? I don't know, but it gave him a lift. I'm his best fucking friend and when something moves him, I can feel it.

She looks at me, her eyes darker than usual, as if she's decided that tomorrow doesn't count until... tomorrow.

I tap my lap demonstratively. A blink of an eye - and she moves.

She is not cautious, does not hesitate, but climbs astride my lap, her lips just millimetres away from mine. I can feel her heartbeat myself. Quickly.

I brush her hair to the side, kiss her where her neck meets her shoulder. A tremor goes through her body. "Val." I don't know if it's a command or a warning but I don't stop.

And then there's Jasper and Layton again, touching her, stroking her skin, caressing her. Three pairs of hands, three different tempos - we all know them, but each in their own way.

Layton is the one who listens to her. The one who waits and looks at her as if she were the most beautiful chaos that has ever entered his life. Jasper tests her. Challenges and provokes her, shows her how much control she has - or doesn't have.

And I am the one who lets her fall. But also the one who holds her when she lets go.

I sink my teeth into her skin - she moans.

Jasper's fingers slide deeper - her hips twitch.

Layton holds her tight. He whispers something in her ear but I only hear fragments. "When it's over..." - "...remember." - "...don't worry."

Her fingers claw into my back and I know I'll feel it the next morning. And I want it. I want every damn mark. Every scratch.

Jasper looks at me and our eyes cross. It's a silent agreement before he pulls her off me and places her on the edge of the couch.

This time Jasper takes care of her mouth, Layton takes care of her breasts, and I penetrate her from behind with a forceful jerk. She doesn't scream, but she makes sounds that go through her body. Half pleasure, half... pain? No, more as if something is bursting out of her that has been hidden for far too long.

Minutes blur. Seconds stretch out. I lose myself. Every now and then I change position without really noticing. It doesn't matter where I am with her. Every part of her makes my heart beat faster. There are words, whole sentences that form in my head but don't pass my lips.

We bathe in the heat and sweat, sliding back and forth on the foil.

Jasper comes first in her mouth, then on her stomach.

Layton pulls his cock out of her before he pours out on her back.

And as everything starts to shake in the final round, she holds on to me. Claws into my chest, pulls me to her, whispers my name.

Then Layton's.

Then Jasper's.

And then - nothing more.

Just breath.

Just a pulse.

Only silence.

And I cum.

19
Firefly

Jasper

The night is silent. Only the soft rustling of leaves in the wind and the chirping of crickets break the darkness. The moon casts a silvery light over the forest and bathes the hut and the small lake in an almost surreal scene.

I should be asleep by now, but something is keeping me awake.

Or rather - someone.

Marra.

We all showered together, scrubbed all the paint off our bodies and then fell asleep together in Marra's bedroom. Only Layton looked for another place to sleep.

I heard it when she got up. The soft squeak of the floorboards, the barely perceptible sound of the door swinging on its hinges. I know she can't sleep. Maybe it's the heat. Maybe it's because the weekend is coming to an end. Maybe it's because of us.

So I follow her.

Neither Val nor Lay have heard us or woken up to follow us. Her small figure moves slowly across the forest floor, barefoot, in a light white shirt and short sleep pants. Her hair falls in soft waves over her shoulders as she walks with her head bowed. I hurriedly put on my shoes and take hers with me, because I'm pretty sure it can get quite cold in the long run.

I don't like it when she's sad.

It's a painful tug in my chest that takes my breath away. I don't want her to feel bad.

Damn, baby, lift your head and jump happily through the forest.

We were trying to make you happy, not second guessing.

She doesn't realize I'm behind her.

Not until I step on a branch.

She flinches, whirls around, her eyes widen, then she exhales. "Bloody hell, Jas." She puts a hand over her heart. "You scared me." I raise my hands placatingly and move closer to her. "I'm sorry, baby. I just thought I'd keep you company for a bit." She looks at me for a moment, as if she's considering whether to send me away. But then she shrugs and turns back around. "Come with me then." I walk alongside her as we continue our walk through the night. I hold out the shoes to her. "I took these with me." She looks at me gratefully and puts them on. After a few meters, we arrive at a small field of fireflies and Marra looks at them for a few minutes. But she doesn't say a word. She just lets her eyes wander over the grass and the flowers, the fireflies and the bushes. When I look at her like this, I can only think of one fitting term: Mother Nature's daughter. She absorbs the landscape and the forest as if it were her life energy. As if that's all she needs to stay fit. She looks at all the fireflies as if each of them gives her hope.

"Can't you sleep?" I finally ask after we've taken a few more steps, breaking the silence that has spread between us. She shakes her head. Her soft hair falls into her face and I gently brush it back behind her ear. "My head is too full." I look at her from the side. Her brow is furrowed slightly, as if she's struggling with a thought she doesn't want to say.

And damn it, I want to burst.

I can't look at her like this any longer.

Every fiber of my being tenses and panics. I want to make her happy again. I don't want her to suffer. I want her to enjoy. Just a few hours ago, she was so relaxed and free. What's happened all of a sudden? Something's changed since she spoke to Layton. Only I don't know what.

"Do you want to tell me what's bothering you?"

She laughs softly, but it's not a happy laugh. It's more like she's making fun of herself. "I don't know what I'm thinking myself."

I wait. I learned in my school days that Marra needs time to open up. That's never changed, and I'm glad it has.

I'm glad she's still the girl I fell in love with back then. Because she made that weekend the best of my life.

And finally, after a few more steps, she lifts her head to the sky and looks up at the stars, as if silently praying for help.

Then she says it.

"I've fallen in love with you."

The sentence hits me harder than I had expected.

I stand still. She does too.

She turns to me, her big brown eyes searching mine. They are full of emotion - uncertainty, pain, hope.

"In all of you," she adds quietly. "And I know that's stupid. I know it's not realistic. But... it happened."

My heart beats faster. I'm thinking so fast I'm about to have a heart attack.

Baby.

My heart breaks a little.

I knew it. Of course I knew it.

But hearing it - hearing it from her mouth - makes it so much harder. She lowers her eyes, kicks a small stone with her foot.

"This weekend was..." She laughs briefly, softer this time, sadder. "It was the craziest thing I've ever done. I broke out of my own little world. I did things I never thought I could do. And I feel alive. Really alive."

She sighs deeply and I have to pull myself together not to shake.

"I'm so incredibly grateful to you. You've given me this chance. I've learned more in these two days than I have in my entire life. None of this would have been possible without you three."

Then she looks at me. With that spark of hope in her eyes that I fear so much.

"I could imagine it," she finally says. "Going to New York with you guys, you know? To try out this life."

My chest tightens painfully.

My heart cries out and I wonder if I'm really ill. That's exactly what we all want, isn't it? But my mind knows better.

Because I have to say exactly what she doesn't want to hear.

"Marra..."

She bites her lip as if she can hold back the words and shut me up. But I can't keep quiet. I'm not allowed to.

"Don't say anything. Just let me explain, okay? After that, you can bring me back to reality."

I take a deep breath.

My chest suddenly feels so tight.

"Yeah, I imagined what it would be like if I just did it. But then I wondered if you even wanted it. Do you want me? The way I am?" She takes a deep breath and apparently that wasn't really a question, because she doesn't wait for an answer. "I've fallen into self-doubt." I want to contradict her and encourage her, I want to tell her that we would love to take her to New York with us, just as she is, the Marra we know.

I want to tell her that everything will be easy.

That we will build a perfect, beautiful life there.

All of us together.

But that would be a lie.

And I won't lie to Marra.

"I know you like me. That you find me somehow... special. And I know that I've also found a part of yourselves that you don't want to lose. I have seen you. The way you really are, because you never had to pretend in front of me. And it was precisely because of your true faces that I fell in love with you all three." She searches my gaze. She's looking for confirmation that I can't give her. I feel bad because she knows nothing. She has no idea what we're really like. What we have become. There are too many things she doesn't know, things that would be important to lead an honest future.

"So, tell me, why can't I go with you?"

It hurts like hell. I close my eyes for a moment and force myself to accept the words I'm about to say myself.

"I don't want you to do this."

She frowns. "What do you mean?"

Her voice is shaky, and it feels like someone is plunging a knife into my stomach and twisting it.

"I mean..." I shake my head, searching for the right words. "You think you want it. Because this weekend felt right. Because we felt right. But you don't really know our life, baby. You've only seen a little slice of it. And it wasn't real."

"What do you mean 'it wasn't real'?"

I remain silent.

Her lips open, but I'm quicker.

"I don't want you to change for us. I don't want you to force yourself into a life that doesn't suit you just because you long to be something else in the moment." She gives me a hurt look, and it tears me up inside. "Jasper, I -"

"You'd hate it." My voice is soft but determined. "The city, the pressure, the speed, the volume, the people there. The way we live. It would break you, Marra. You would lose yourself. And that's the last thing I want." I can see the tears welling up in her eyes, her fingers clawing at her top.

"As soon as you see our lives, our plans, our ambitions... We are fast. Brave."

Her face reflects astonishment and she tilts her head. "And me? I love the silence. I love nature. I love it when I can stop time instead of running after it. And is it such a big problem for you that I can't live with you? Would I just slow you down?"

She looks at me as if I've insulted her to the ground. I wipe my face and shake my head in despair. "No, baby. We like you just the way you are. You're perfect, believe me. And you certainly wouldn't stop us, but New York - that would only destroy you. You just said yourself what you love. And those things don't exist in our lives. And you wouldn't be able to cope with that."

"That's not for you to decide. You don't have to cut me any slack. I'm not a little kid, I already know what I'm getting myself into."

I look at her sympathetically because she's so upset, so emotional, that she doesn't even know what she's thinking anymore. I can see it on her face. She is confused and overwhelmed. Her eyes are flickering, her chest is shaking and her fingers are trembling. She no longer knows what is right and what is wrong, can no longer distance herself from the misperception of her feelings. She has no control over her feelings, her feelings control her.

She can't assess herself.

"I love you."

My throat constricts.

I run my hand through my hair and look up at the sky for a moment because otherwise it would be too hard to look at her. Then I exhale and say the words I never wanted to say.

"And I love you. We all do. But it's not enough."

She shivers.

"Why not?"

I look at her. My gaze is gentle, my eyes burning.

"Because love doesn't always mean it works."

A single tear rolls down her cheek. She hastily wipes it away, takes a deep breath. "Baby, there's nothing in New York that can hold you. Nothing you love. Nothing that can make you happy."

"You're all there." I put a hand to her cheek and she nuzzles it.

"You're not the kind of woman who gets emotionally dependent on men, baby. You're so much stronger and better than that. And that's exactly what it would be like if you went to New York just for us and tried to stay: Dependence. And I don't want to put that burden on you."

Another tear rolls down her cheek and this time I intercept it with my finger. She looks pale.

"I wish it were different," I finally say quietly. "I wish we had met again under different circumstances. At a different point in our lives." But this is all my fault. I knew we would meet her here again. I set out to do it. I made this deal with her - it was me who promised her a vision of this weekend that I might not be able to keep now.

She swallows hard and more tears gather in her eyes.

"Yeah, me too."

I bite the inside of my cheeks painfully, trying to stop myself from making false promises to this woman. I want to make her happy and it tears me apart that I can't.

Then she nods. A single, slow nod.

"I understand."

I want to say something, want to explain to her that it hurts me just as much. That I would like it as much as she does. I want to tell her more than 'I wish it were different'. But what good would it do?

The silence between us is heavy, laden with all the words we can't say.

So I do the only thing I can.

I have made this agreement with her. I have to finish it too.

I take a step towards her and my heart leaps painfully as she takes a step towards me at the same time, as if our thoughts are intertwined. I wrap my arms around her and she presses tightly against me, I hold her as if I could stop time. I breathe in her scent deeply, enjoying her soft skin, her soft hair and the way her small body nestles against my big one. She buries her face against my chest and breathes me in too, as if she wants to memorize this moment. I want a better life for her. Not a Val who isn't honest with her. Not one like Layton and me who won't come clean about a lie and just live with it.

I kiss the crown of her head. Then I whisper into her hair:

"I'll always miss you."

I want to hold her in my arms forever.

Because I know it will be the last hug.

She says nothing. Because there's nothing more to say.

And I let her go.

20

Paparazzi

Marra

*I*t starts with a noise.
A low hum, barely more than a tremor in the silence.

I'm lying on my side, the blanket pulled halfway over me, my face buried in the pillow. My thoughts are floating somewhere between dream and reality, and I'm so exhausted that I ignore the noise for the time being.

Hum.

It doesn't stop.

Muffled and eerie.

I squint into the darkness of the room, which is only lit by the faint moonlight. Somewhere nearby, a telephone is vibrating - not mine, I know that. I haven't touched mine for two days and it's still in my bag.

Hum.

With a soft sigh, I turn around and look for the source of the noise. My eyes are still sticky and puffy from the tears I shed earlier on the secret walk between Jasper and me. My chest still feels empty, somehow bereft. As if all my passion had been stolen from me.

I wanted to say goodbye to Val and Lay right away and go home, but Jasper told me not to. He wanted me to sleep on it one more night, try to calm down and not leave until the next morning. He took me back to the house safely, but I lay down in the living room while Jas went back to Val's bedroom.

The look he gave me as he left me here alone will haunt my worst nightmares. It was pity. The ultimate in pity. There was guilt. And sadness.

I felt his own pain. But that doesn't make it any better.

Hum.

I straighten up and look at the kitchen table, where the culprit lies.

It's Valerian's phone. The display lights up and a name flashes out at me as I get up and walk towards it.

Izabella.

I stare at the display and the name.

Something tightens in my chest, a dull pressure that I can't name. Izabella. I know that name. She's a friend from New York, isn't she? The one from the bar.

Hum.

I don't know why I'm staring at the phone for so long. Maybe because it feels like it means more than it should. As if this name isn't just any name. When the display finally goes dark again, I force myself to look away.

But then suddenly short text messages appear, all from Izabella, one after the other. I reach for the satellite phone, pull out the antenna and stare at the display.

Izabella: Call me.
Izabella: They've seen you.
Izabella: You're just causing problems.
Izabella: Who the hell is she?
Izabella: Come home.

I put it down again with a queasy feeling and try to stop myself from thinking negatively. But what does that mean? Who is she? And why does she call Valerian so often in the middle of the night?

I can't sleep any more.

Maybe it's the humming, maybe it's the last few days, maybe it's the realization that it's coming to an end or the conversation with Jasper. I don't know exactly. My bag is on the dresser in the hallway. I reach for my phone, it's a second-hand, old satellite phone that my mother got for me through a colleague at work. However, I can only use it to send text messages, which is why I switch it on - and I immediately see the countless messages that have piled up over the last few days. Which is strange, because I don't know many people who send me a text message just like that.

My mother, who gets in touch to let me know that everything is fine with Leo. But then my stomach tightens as my eyes fall on one particular message.

Dana: Check the celebrity portal.
Dana: Is that you in the photo?
Dana: Next to Valerian?

It's not just the strange feeling that comes over me at the urgency of her words, but also the fact that Dana never messages me. I spoke to her at the reunion for the first time in a long time.

My heart beats faster.

I go to Jasper's travel bag and pull out his laptop with modem, place it on the kitchen island in no time at all and switch it on.

I bounce my legs impatiently, bite the edges of my fingernails and somehow try to convince myself that everything is fine.

Is it?

I haven't the faintest idea.

When the screen finally lights up, I open the internet, search for the celebrity portal and follow the fat bar with my eyes, which only moves within ten seconds. And then only minimally.

Hum.

It's another call from Izabella.

My heart almost leaps as the bar is almost finished and the pixelated image slowly dissolves. The connection out here is weak but still good enough.

And then I see the new headline. Below it is a poor resolution image, black and white and a little blurred but you can still make out a lot.

Too much, if you ask me.

I see myself.

That's me.

A photo taken at Jadie's wedding. It shows the moment when Jas, Val and I run away from Jadie. Valerian very close to me. His lively gaze is passionately focused on me. His hand is around my wrist, my hair is tousled from the wind and our sex, my face is half in shadow. But you can see what we've been up to.

The accompanying text burns painfully into my retina.

New York's famous up-and-coming stockbroker Valerian King as a guest at a wedding. His date? Not his fiancée, anyway. Does the impending marriage already seem to be on the rocks? What will his future wife Izabella St. James say? And even more interesting: Who is his mysterious affair?

My heart stops.

My head is spinning.

Fiancée?

My fingers go numb, my vision blurs. I blink hastily and try to read the words again, hoping that I'm wrong, that it says something else - but no.

Valerian is engaged.

And I'm not just anyone in this picture. I am the woman who is portrayed as a threat. As an affair.

I feel sick.

The air suddenly feels far too thin, my chest shrinks to the size of a pea. The buzzing of Valerian's phone snaps me out of my daze.

Izabella.

Suddenly everything becomes clear to me.

They met in the bar and fell in love.

She's not just any old friend.

Izabella isn't just any old name.

Izabella is his fiancée.

And he never told me.

He never told me the truth.

Tears of anger gather in my eyes, and I claw at my hair, pulling so hard my scalp burns. I feel as if the ground has been pulled out from under my feet and all that lies beneath me is a deep emptiness into which I fall with no end in sight.

I run up the stairs as if in a trance, knocking everything over and sounding like a clumsy animal. But I don't care.

I don't give a shit about anything.

How can he do this to me?

My heart is pounding as I slam the door behind me. My lungs are burning, not from running, but from breathing. From trying to gasp for air while my whole chest feels like it's going to burst under the weight of a thousand tons. "Valerian!" My scream cuts through the silence. Then I kick the bed. Even his tired body must sense that something is wrong, because he sits up bolt upright and doesn't even need to wipe the tiredness from his eyes - he's wide awake. The same goes for Jasper, who swings himself out of bed and stands awkwardly by.

"What the hell?" His voice is sleepy, but as he looks at me more closely, something changes in his expression. I turn away as my heart takes a stab.

I stand there, my hands clenched into fists, my knuckles white with tension. My whole body is shaking.

I fling both phones onto the bed. On one he can see Dana's messages, on the other, those of his... fiancée.

It bounces against Val's chest and falls into the blanket next to him. The door opens behind me, Layton sticks his head into the room and then closes it behind him. He stands beside me, looking at me for a moment, but I don't have the strength to look at him.

"Take it," I groan, turning to Valerian. "Read it."

He reaches for it, looks at the screen - and then I see it. The minimal narrowing of his eyes, the barely noticeable stiffening of his fingers. "Marra, I can explain." His voice is panicked.

Layton joins Jasper at the edge of the bed, Valerian still sitting in it, eyes lowered, hands clasped.

And me?

I'm the storm in this room.

I laugh out, but it's a cold, broken sound. "Then explain to me why your name is in a fucking article with fiancée!"

Silence.

The other two also seem to have realized what this is all about, because they look contritely at Valerian and then sadly at me. I can't look them in the eye. I'm so ashamed to have been so stupid. So, so stupid.

Finally, I turn to them, my gaze angry and disappointed. "You knew." My voice shakes. "You all knew." Jasper rubs his face tiredly, Layton looks to the ground.

"Marra..." Layton starts to explain, but I throw my arms up.

"No, don't talk yourselves out of it! You've got to be kidding me!"

I can feel myself shaking, but I force myself not to give in. Not now.

I bang the flat of my hand against the doorframe. "You lied to me." I told Jasper I loved them. And damn it, I do. Something inside of me, the dumbest, stupidest part of me, has decided to fall in love with them. And I hate myself so much for it right now that I don't just want to rip their heads off, I want to rip my own off too.

"Baby..." Jasper begins, but I jerk my head around and stare at him. "Don't talk to me like I'm a fucking child, Jasper! Like I'm stupid and naïve and don't understand any of this!" I shake my head, my voice breaking. "For fuck's sake, I get it. I understood it better than you could ever explain it to me."

I point at Valerian. "You're engaged." The word tastes like poison on my tongue. "And you didn't tell me. You all didn't tell me, but dragged me into this shit when I knew nothing about it!"

"Because it means nothing!" interjects Valerian. His voice is louder than mine, his gaze pleading. "Dammit, Marra, Izabella is-it's complicated. This engagement isn't real. This engagement is... For business reasons, okay? I don't love her."

I laugh bitterly. "You still didn't say it. Not a single word. Do you think that makes it less of a betrayal? Towards me? Let alone to her? Does your fiancée know what you're doing here?"

He presses his lips together and I can see it working in his head. Silence.

That's what I thought.

Jasper sighs and steps forward. "Marra, listen to me. We didn't mean to hurt you."

"But you did." I close my eyes, fluttering. "You hurt me, Jasper. Because you decided I couldn't handle the truth. Because you decided it would be better if I stayed stupid. And you know what? I've experienced this my whole life. People making decisions about me and thinking they know what's good for me. That they're keeping me down." A tear rolls down my cheek. "I thought this was real. But it's not."

"It is!" Valerian stands up, his shoulders tense. "This - this is real." I snort. "Really?" I try to blink away more tears. "It would have been real if you'd told me the truth. But you didn't. You took advantage of me."

"Marra, please," Jasper murmurs. I can feel how much this situation is hurting him. But it hurts me even more. "It wasn't like that..."

"Shut up, Jasper!" I shout, looking at him contritely. "Is that what you meant when you said earlier that I wouldn't feel comfortable in your lives? Because your life is all lies? Is that what's normal for you? Is it okay for you to cheat on an engagement just because it's business? Is it okay for you to hurt people?" I laugh derisively. "I was talking about how nice it is to see your real faces. That I fell in love with you. I felt honored to know the real men behind their new, expensive suits. But it was all a lie and a fake. You had me by the nose."

His face twitches as if I've hit him.

I take a deep breath and try to suppress the trembling of my hands.

"I knew it was just a weekend. No promises. No consequences. Just us, no rules, no expectations. I gave in to it. I gave in to it because I thought we were being honest with each other." My chest tightens. They lied to me and underestimated me because they thought I was the fragile little girl. And that hurts more than anything.

I look directly at Valerian, his gaze is heavy, full of unspoken things. But that's not important. It doesn't matter if he loves Izabella or not.

"Marriage of convenience or not. You betrayed her, Valerian. And me too. I thought this weekend would be about three men who need to clear their heads, about a woman who finally wants to rise above herself. But instead you turned me into a naive deer and got me caught up in a lie, in an affair."

I take a few steps forward and feel my throat tighten. "And the worst part?"

My voice softens, almost breaks, barely audible. "You thought I was just this good, innocent girl who doesn't know what she wants. The one who always stays in the shadows, who never dares to step out of line. The little Marra who's too fragile to make it in the outside world." Layton looks like he wants to protest, but I won't let him.

"You've seen in me the Marra that everyone else sees in me. The one I sometimes even see in myself, but tried to break out of while I thought you were seeing the real Marra."

I shake my head coldly.

"I'm not someone to be spared. I got involved in something I really wanted. Which, however, was obviously a lie from the start. And I hate lies." I turn to Jasper and Layton. "You made this weekend palatable to me, you gave me the courage to push my boundaries. And at the same time, you betrayed me just like he did." My gaze shifts to Valerian.

"I thought I was finally free. I thought I was finally fully wanted. But I was just another secret sin in Valerian King's life."

I realize how hard my words are for them all. But I don't care. They have to live with the consequences. They've ripped my heart out of my chest. Just a few hours ago, Jasper and Layton would have had the opportunity to tell me in confidence. Our conversations were intimate and characterized by truth. At least that's what I thought. But even then, they betrayed me.

"Marra, I'm sorry."

Valerian's apology rushes past me as if he hadn't even said it. I stare absently at the wall behind them, trying to get my heart to keep on living and beating at a normal, healthy pace. "Star?"

I don't answer.

And then all my nerves snap.

I just shit on it.

"I got a diagnosis when I was sixteen. Avoidant personality disorder. Do you know what that means?"

Silence. I did know. My words lie in the room like a veil of lead. The men look at me desperately.

"It means that I've hidden from the world because I always think I'm not good enough. That I never dared to want anything because the fear of rejection was greater than anything else. It means that every time I looked at you - as a teenager and now - I knew I would never be brave enough to do what I really wanted."

Valerian closes his eyes briefly, Layton looks down at the floor, Jasper clenches his jaw. I laugh softly, but it sounds insane. "Until this weekend." I force myself not to let the tears well up again, even though I'm breaking up inside. "For the first time, I dared to do something for myself. For the first time, I surprised myself. And then - then you ruin it with a lie." I look at the faces of the three men I thought were my freedom. Who I fell in love with, even though I knew from the start that I shouldn't. Who made me believe for a moment that I could be more than the girl who only ever dreams but never acts.

"I could have somehow lived with the fact that it was just a weekend. But not with the lie. Not with the fact that you underestimated me as much as everyone else."

Jasper raises a hand as if to reach for me, but I back away.

I'm breathing heavily. It makes me angry that I have so much to say about this, but all they do is look at me guiltily, like they're just accepting this pain. They can't be serious, can they?

"I thought we were friends. More than that."

"We are!" Valerian blurts out.

"Friends don't lie to each other!" I shout back.

Silence.

I see Valerian clench his hands into fists, his jaw so tight it's almost vibrating.

Jasper's gaze is full of guilt and pain. "We wanted to protect you," he says quietly.

From themselves? From the lies and deceit they themselves caused? I shake my head. "But why don't you understand? I don't need protection. I need honesty. I need people to tell me what's what instead of treating me like some stupid, clueless thing." Valerian rubs his face. "Marra, I'm so sorry. This is all my fault. Please..." He pauses and swallows hard. "Please let's sort this out properly. Don't let the weekend end like this. You mean at least as much to us as we do to you." I swallow hard and lean against the cold door of the room.

"I can't. I can't live with people like you in a world that's so ... wrong. A world that keeps destroying me. Jasper was absolutely right." My heart aches. My chest feels like it's about to burst. Every breath is heavy and feels like a new weight is always being added, compressing my lungs. My body feels numb and dizzy, there is a throbbing behind my forehead. I would like to let my legs give way underneath me so that I can just fall to the ground and not have to hold on anymore. But my body feels cramped, like it's stuck in one position. I can't move a muscle or lift a finger.

Valerian stands up, wipes his face in despair. I stand still, looking at him - unable to do anything else. The shock settles deep into my bones and prevents me from showing any reaction.

My heart stops beating.

"I love you, Marra Flores. Part of me never stopped. I left this town because I was a coward, because I was looking for something to give me courage. Coming here after all these years and seeing you again has awakened something in me. My last spark of humanity flared up again. And I didn't hesitate or think for a second. I wanted you more than anything, starlet, and I still do. I'm sorry." I can't look at him, it hurts too much.

I wish I could believe his words. But even if I did, they wouldn't change anything, would they?

"Ever since I saw you again, I've thought of nothing but you. You're everything I long for and you're everything I want in my life. You are the one I need. Not because of your body or your looks. But because of the way you are. Because of the way you've always seen and loved me without really knowing me. You are so pure and beautiful that it scares me beyond belief. And I'm sorry I was such a coward and ruined this chance."

I let Valerian's words sink in and it seems the others do too. I have a lump in my throat that won't go away, no matter how often and how hard I swallow. And the burning in my eyes doesn't diminish. I want to love him for these words. I want to stay with him, I want to forgive him for all this drama. I want to go to New York with him, Jasper, and Layton.

But that's not what I choose for myself. Fuck it. That's what I should have done in the first place. No matter how painful it is.

I've learned my lesson.

I'm not choosing Layton Reed.

Not Jasper Bailey.

And not Valerian King either.

And certainly not New York.

I'm choosing me.

"We never had a chance you could ruin." My voice is cool and emotionless as I lift my gaze. "You have a fiancée at home waiting for you." Valerian's gaze breaks. He looks at me with all the pain and self-loathing he must carry inside. Suddenly I feel nothing but pity. He has a fiancée he doesn't love. He has lost the woman he really has feelings for and who is also in love with him. And he only has himself to blame for that. Despite everything, the last living part of my heart dissolves when I see him so broken and destroyed. His gaze begs me.

Please don't.

But I turn away and look at Layton.

He tries to give me a brave smile, straightens his shoulders. But I can see the sadness and tiredness in his eyes. They don't light up, they look dead. "I'm sorry I let you down, little Mar." I swallow hard and look to the last.

Jasper seems to have understood what I've decided in my head. He's always been the best at understanding me. His eyes are shining - a sign that he too is moved to tears and deeply hurt. But then he nods weakly at me. He encourages me in my decision. And despite my anger, I am infinitely grateful to him.

I look at them, the three men who mean more to me than anyone else in my life. And then I say the words that will take everything away from me.

"I'm leaving."

And no one stops me.

Epilogue

Layton

The elevator doors of our penthouse close behind us and Jasper throws his travel bag away. It skids across the slippery floor until it hits the wall and stays there.

He whirls through the apartment with quick steps, running from room to room as if he's organizing things in his head. I walk leisurely into the bright kitchen, take a glass from the cupboard and fill it up with cold water. Then I lean against the counter and take a sip.

We didn't speak a word on the flight back. There's not much to say either. There's no explanation for what happened a few hours ago.

I think back to Valerian, watching Marra with cold and broken eyes as she packed her things and left the cabin. She didn't look at him once. I'm drunk. Bought myself so much alcohol on the flight I can't count it on two hands. Not even on four.

"Bloody hell," Jas yells and the next thing I hear is one of the expensive vases thundering onto the floor. Shards whizz across the floor.

He steps back into my field of vision, his hair disheveled and his gaze torn. Two corner sofas face each other in the middle of the room, with several stools and small glass tables between them. Behind them, a staircase leads to the upper floor. He slumps down on one of the sofas, lets his head sink back and buries his face in his hands.

I drink more water.

My head is throbbing numbly and my vision is slightly blurred.

How could it have come to this? How could I have allowed us to hurt her so badly? I didn't realize the extent of this secret. I didn't realize it was even relevant. But Marra was right about everything - her every word has been like a slap of reality. My heart clenches and I close my eyes sadly.

Jasper takes the cap off his head and throws it at the nearest vase. This also shatters into a thousand pieces.

He warned me in advance. Asked me what we would do if it did become our problem. I didn't want to believe that Marra was really ready for more. But the whole atmosphere changed. There were feelings involved. There were words and feelings for each of us.

I didn't believe that this weekend would be our undoing. He warned me. And I was stupid, completely blinded.

Marra's feelings *are* our problem, because we caused the pain. She was ready to stay with us. No matter how hard it would have been, it's always worth a try. But we destroyed everything.

It's not Marra who thinks naively and thoughtlessly.

It's us.

Me, we are naive. Because we thought we could get away with it. Because we thought it wasn't worth mentioning.

I shake my head silently.

Oh - how wrong we were.

Footsteps sound on the marbled floor and a woman steps to the top of the stairs. Her long brown curls hang down to her hips, her brown eyes dull and expressionless. She has no make-up, freshly made up for bed. She is wearing her silky, champagne-colored pyjamas - consisting of an open shirt and shorts, except for the last two buttons.

Her bare feet plod down the steps, her skin soft and flawless, as always. Her toes are polished, her fingernails manicured, her lips moisturized with creamy balm.

"Where is he?" Her voice is harsh and I can hear the anger and disappointment in it. Izabella has become a good friend to Jas and me over the years. Perhaps even a best friend. The betrayal affects her not only from Val, but also from us.

It's a similar feeling to Marra.

Except that I don't love Izabella. Not the way I learned to love Marra.

Jasper rises angrily from the couch and shakes his head in disbelief. She stops at the landing, her arms crossed in front of her chest, her eyes scrutinizing and analyzing. "You're drunk," she states, her voice even more bitter than before.

I don't want to upset her, I don't want to stab her in the back. But it's too late for either and I'm in no position to say anything. We have failed.

"I'll ask one last time. Where is he?"

I look helplessly at Jas. He stops in front of the huge window and looks out at New York, his eyes shining, his chest tense. "Not here."

She laughs derisively. "I can see that for myself, thank you very much dearest Sherlock Bailey." Jasper seems to come to his senses and gives her an apologetic look.

He is exasperated.

"He stayed there," I say, grumbling, coming out of my safe cave, the kitchen.

"In Asheville?" I nod. She takes a deep breath, shaky and puzzled. Her forehead wrinkles, her body shakes a little.

But she says nothing more. She looks back and forth between Jas and me, seems to be thinking carefully about what she's going to do next. Then she sits down on the couch and gestures for us to join her. I stagger and clear my throat to regain a little control. Then I drop down opposite her. Jas next to me. She looks at us like a worried but angry mother looks at her children, her hands placed gently in her lap.

Then she swallows hard. "Are you all right?"

I'm surprised by this question.

What Valerian said is true. He and Iza are engaged because of their status. After several years of a great friendship, it was the most logical thing for both of them. They have deep feelings for each other, I won't deny that, but they're not the kind of feelings a married couple should have. Izabella owes him nothing and she got involved anyway because she wanted to help her best friend.

She gave up a lot for him. I can well understand her anger at this betrayal. She feels betrayed and rightly so.

And now the culprit isn't even here to explain himself to her or apologize to her.

And despite everything, she's interested in our well-being?

I sigh heavily. "We feel bad. About a lot of things."

She shrugs her shoulders. "That's nothing new, you guys do shit all the time. But I'm asking you, are you okay?"

Jas shakes his head.

She tilts her head.

"And is he okay?"

I give Jas a look and press my lips tightly together. Val is not fine.

He's stayed there, trying to fight for something he lost long ago. The game is over, all the chess pieces have fallen.

Jas shakes his head again.

Izabella nods curtly and cracks her knuckles. Snorts and leans back, her curls framing her face like a work of love. She is Sicilian, quick-tempered and spirited - but just as passionate and loving. But I can't see any of that right now. She has put on a perfect mask of dislike and disinterest, looking at us dismissively.

"Good, and you can be sure - I'm going to make you feel even worse for a while."

Acknowledgments

Writing books is an exhausting, chaotic, nerve-wracking and often heartbreaking process - but there are people who make it less dark.

It is these people that I would like to thank, because they have made the last few months a lot easier for me.

First of all, I would like to thank my family, my mom Conny, who always listens to my ideas and my stories about new books without complaining. My dad, Chrissi, who despite his uncreative streak and stressful job always finds time to put up with my chatter. You put up with the mess in my room and my constant oversleeping when there was too much chaos in my head to get involved in other things. Without you and your support, this book would have remained nothing more than a ball of wool made up of jumbled thoughts. However, I do have one request: I am still your little princess. Please just skip the... scenes. :)

A huge thank you goes out to Michelle, my tireless test reader who gave me merciless feedback and recruited me on her social media channels. I am so grateful to have met you! I would also like to thank my private friends, because they were always eager to find out if there was any news yet and gave me incredible encouragement and support! Laura, who laid the foundations of this story with me. Oumaira, Emana and Lilith, who were always at least as excited and enthusiastic as I was when my project came up. Last but not least - Selin, with her incredible artistic talent. She helped me visualize scenes and went through many ideas with me. Thank you for your support!

To my readers - especially those who are interested in darkness - thank you. Your support on TikTok and Instagram helps me tremendously and means more to me than I could ever put into words.

And finally, thank you to my characters, who kept me awake for hours and made me doubt my own sanity until their story was finished. Or... not quite finished.

With dark (but quite sweet) love,
Amaya Lowell

Trigger Warning – Content Note

This novella contains mature and potentially distressing content intended for adult readers (18+).

Please be advised that Don't Look Back includes depictions of:

- consensual but explicit sexual content (including group intimacy)

- emotional manipulation

- mental health themes (including avoidant personality disorder)

- betrayal and secrecy in close relationships

- temporary emotionally imbalanced dynamics

- references to substance use (alcohol, cigarettes)

- themes of loss, identity, and inner conflict

While all sexual content is consensual, the emotional setting may be intense and layered.

If you are sensitive to any of the above themes, please read with care. Your well-being matters more than any story.

You want more?

Check out all my social media channels to stay up to date
- because there's a lot more to come! That's a promise.
Thank you so much for your support!

Instagram:
@amayalowellauthor
@rewikanempire

TikTok:
@amayalowell
@rewikanempire

Pinterest:
@littlenightrain

bio.site/lowellworld

Do you need a cover designer? Then I might have
something for you.
@mariellalowell - TikTok
@mariellalowelldesign - Instagram